D0612734

ONCE UPON A MIDNIGHT EERIE

The Misadventures of Edgar & Allan Poe

The Tell-Tale Start

Once Upon a Midnight Eerie

ONCE UPON A MIDNIGHT EERIE

Gordon McAlpine
illustrations by Sam Zuppardi

VIKING
An Imprint of Penguin Group (USA)

VIKING
Published by the Penguin Group
Penguin Group (USA) LLC
375 Hudson Street
New York, New York 10014

USA / Canada / UK / Ireland / Australia / New Zealand / India / South Africa / China

penguin.com
A Penguin Random House Company

First published in the United States of America by Viking, an imprint of Penguin Young Readers Group, 2014

Text copyright © 2014 by Gordon McAlpine
Illustrations copyright © 2014 by Sam Zuppardi

Penguin supports copyright. Copyright fuels creativity, encourages diverse voices, promotes free speech, and creates a vibrant culture. Thank you for buying an authorized edition of this book and for complying with copyright laws by not reproducing, scanning, or distributing any part of it in any form without permission. You are supporting writers and allowing Penguin to continue to publish books for every reader.

LIBRARY OF CONGRESS CATALOGING-IN-PUBLICATION DATA
McAlpine, Gordon.
Once upon a midnight eerie / Gordon McAlpine ; illustrations by Sam Zuppardi.
pages cm. — (The misadventures of Edgar and Allan Poe ; book two)
ISBN 978-0-670-78493-6 (hardcover)
[1. Brothers—Fiction. 2. Twins—Fiction. 3. Motion pictures—Production and direction—Fiction. 4. Poe, Edgar Allan, 1809–1849—Fiction. 5. New Orleans (La.)—Fiction.]
I. Zuppardi, Sam, illustrator. II. Title.
PZ7.M11735Onc 2014
[Fic]—dc23
2013014710

Printed in the U.S.A.

10 9 8 7 6 5 4 3 2 1

Designed by Eileen Savage
Set in Stempel Schneidler

To Don Zappia—G.M.

To Dad—S.Z.

Lettin' the cat outta the bag is

a whole lot easier than puttin' it back in.

—Will Rogers

CONTENTS

ONCE UPON A MIDNIGHT EERIE

New Orleans Daily Post, Entertainment Section, D-1

HERO TWINS TO SHOOT MOVIE IN NEW ORLEANS

Pictured above: Edgar and Allan Poe (inset: the boys' famous forebear, Edgar Allan Poe, circa. 1835)

NEW ORLEANS, LA. — Fresh from their recent capture of the dangerous criminal S. Pangborn Perry (a.k.a. Professor Marvel), twelve-year-old twins Edgar and Allan Poe have agreed to appear in the new movie, *A Tale of Poe*. The movie, to be directed by famed German director Werner Wender, will shoot scenes here in New Orleans and will revolve around the life of Edgar Allan Poe, the nineteenth-century American author renowned for his tales of horror and mystery. Young Edgar and Allan, who bear a striking resemblance to the famous author, are Mr. Poe's actual great-great-great-great grandnephews and will play him as a boy in two scenes.

"We don't have any previous movie acting experience," Edgar explained in a phone interview with this newspaper.

"But then we didn't have any previous experience when it came to apprehending criminals and yet we did okay with Professor Perry and his henchmen," Allan added.

Police in Kansas describe the boys' crime-fighting activities two weeks ago at a run-down theme park called the Dorothy Gale Farm and OZitorium as being little short of miraculous.

"And to think they did it

all while disguised as flying monkeys!" added police chief John J. Stanley. Nonetheless, the boys have brushed off most of the praise, explaining that their primary intent was just to rescue their cat (named Roderick Usher, in tribute to the character in Poe's "The Fall of the House of Usher"), who had been stolen from their home in Baltimore by the master criminal Professor S. Pangborn Perry. Why a criminal of such dark repute would commit as trivial-seeming a crime as catnapping remains a mystery about which the Poe twins, their guardians, and the authorities offer no comment. As for Professor Perry's recent escape from Kansas authorities, Edgar and Allan Poe remain unafraid.

"Now that his cover is blown and his hideout has been exposed, he's on the run, someplace far, far away," said Edgar.

Interpol and the F.B.I. report recent sightings of Professor Perry in Shanghai and Hong Kong.

ON THE AIR

AT 5:55 in the morning, long before anyone should be out of bed, Edgar and Allan Poe sat on tall swivel chairs three miles apart at the TV studios of New Orleans's two top morning shows. At WKEU, the makeup artist for *Rise and Shine, New Orleans!* applied layers of greasy gunk onto Edgar's face. Meanwhile, stagehands across town at the studios of WJRT's *Wake Up, New Orleans!* pinched and poked at Allan's back and shoulders to attach a battery pack and wireless microphone beneath his jacket.

"Five minutes to airtime," stage managers shouted at each of the stations.

Edgar and Allan watched from the wings as battalions of crew members in each studio put on wireless headsets and took positions behind cameras, lights, microphone booms, or control boards. The two sound stages became even more hectic when the shows' smiling hosts (at WKEU, a man with good hair; at WJRT, a woman with excellent posture) emerged from their dressing rooms. The hosts made their ways onto their similarly cheerful sets, where each was met like royalty by eager assistants.

What a grandiose production, Edgar thought.

Across town in the other studio, Allan agreed with his brother. *Grandiose is just the half of it,* he observed. *You'd think this was the opening ceremony of the Olympics, instead of just a show for people to watch while they eat their cornflakes.*

Across town, Edgar chuckled under his breath. *Or if not cornflakes, strawberry pancakes,* he added to the psychic conversation.

Strawberry pancakes were the boys' favorite.

Yum . . . Allan murmured ravenously.

They hadn't eaten breakfast yet.

"Two minutes to airtime! Places, everybody!"

"You ready to put on a good show, Edgar?" a production assistant at WKEU asked.

"All set to brighten up New Orleans, Allan?" asked a WJRT assistant.

"Sure, why not?" the boys answered, identically and with perfect synchronization. (Of course, no one knew this except the Poe twins, who remained in one another's minds at all times, even when they were physically apart.)

Yes, even for identical twins, Edgar and Allan were unusual.

The boys' uncle and aunt, Jack and Judith Poe—who had remained back at the hotel to watch the broadcasts, having bundled their nephews off when the limousines from the TV stations arrived—thought of them simply as clever boys with overactive imaginations and a taste for mischief.

But that wasn't the whole story.

The boys' friends back in Baltimore thought Edgar and Allan were not only the smartest and oddest pair in school, but also the most valuable when it came to livening things up with pranks.

That wasn't the whole story, either.

Ironically, the most astute description of the boys might have come from Professor S. Pangborn Perry, their archnemesis. Professor Perry had been observing Edgar and Allan since they were born—first, he'd observed as a legitimate researcher, and then, when the boys' parents forbade him from seeing them, as a spy tracking their every movement.

Professor Perry knew this:

Edgar and Allan Poe were so alike that not only was it impossible for others to tell them apart, but even the twins didn't see themselves as separate boys. One moment one was Edgar, the next he was Allan. Whatever one knew, the other also knew; whatever one saw, the other saw simultaneously. The boys could not explain how their two brains worked as one or how such perfect coordination had come to be.

Regardless, this connection ensured that the twins' deductive and imaginative powers exceeded even the high expectations placed on them as descendants and namesakes of one of America's most brilliant nineteenth-century writers.

It also meant that Professor Perry—who theorized that their connection had something to do with quantum physics—wanted to kidnap them, killing one and keeping the other captive to use as a channel of communication from this world to the world of the dead.

At six a.m., a red light glowed atop a TV camera in each of the two studios. Recorded theme music blared and big, electronic signs overhead snapped to life, reading:

Moments later, the host at WKEU announced: *"Rise and Shine, New Orleans!* It's another beautiful day in the Crescent City. And here's our first guest, Edgar Poe."

"Wake Up, New Orleans!" cried the hostess at WJRT. "Have you got your café au lait? It's my pleasure to introduce Allan Poe."

The boys walked onto their respective sets, taking their seats.

"Young Edgar here is the great-great-great-great grandnephew of that creepy author Edgar Allan Poe," the TV host said. . . .

Creepy?

While simultaneously, the other host said to her morning audience, "Young Allan here is a descendant of Poe, the writer who many thought was crazy. . . ."

Crazy?

The twins didn't tolerate insults to their famous ancestor.

So, in the blink of an eye, they concocted a plan.

"Welcome to the show, Edgar," said the host at WKEU, his fake grin half a foot wide. "It's exciting news about the movie you and your brother will be shooting here. Tell our audience who's directing the film. I think they'll be quite impressed."

Edgar nodded. "A delicious little crawfish in spicy gumbo."

This is how the host responded: "What?"

What neither the host nor the confused WKEU audience could know was that seconds before, across town at WJRT, the hostess had said to Allan:

"Being a native of New Orleans and quite proud of our famous restaurants, I always like to start interviews by asking folks what they ate last night for dinner."

Hence, Edgar's answer at the other TV station.

And Allan's answer to the question about what he ate for dinner: "Mr. Werner Wender, award-winning filmmaker."

The hostess's posture slipped a little, as the host's smile had dimmed. But being professionals, they gathered their composure and carried on.

"OK," the host at WKEU continued, glancing down at his notes. "Let's move on to another subject, Edgar. Why don't you tell our audience what you and your brother did to that criminal you captured up in Kansas."

Edgar smiled warmly. "We rolled him over and rubbed his belly until he purred," he said.

"You *what*?" the host exclaimed.

Moments before, across town, this had been the question:

"You and your brother rescued your cat recently," the hostess at WJRT said. "That must have felt good. I'm a cat lover, too. Tell me, what did you do with your kitty when you finally got him back, safe and sound?"

"Oh, we knocked him unconscious and then had him arrested and tossed into prison," Allan answered.

The hostess's face went pale.

The twins fought back identical smiles.

"OK, Edgar," said the WKEU host, in desperation, "let's try something a little more straightforward. You're the great-great-great-great grandnephew of the author Edgar Allan Poe, and I know you're a big fan of his writing. Tell our audience which of his characters you find the most terrifying."

"Actually, three come to mind," Edgar said thoughtfully.

"Albert Einstein, Leonardo da Vinci, and Donald Duck."

The host gritted his perfect teeth, not knowing that a moment before at WJRT the hostess had asked:

"Do you have any role models, Allan?"

"Sure," Allan said, his eyes gleaming. "It's that guy who commits a murder and hides the body under the floor, only to start hearing his victim's heartbeat grow louder and louder until he finally goes insane and confesses to his crime. You know, from our great-great-great-great granduncle's story 'The Tell-Tale Heart.'"

The hostess looked truly alarmed. "Well, um . . . That's enough questions, I guess. More than enough, actually. Thank you for the interview, Allan."

"I'm Edgar," he told her.

She narrowed her eyes. "I thought you were Allan."

He shrugged. "Yes, him, too."

She shook her head, confused.

While across town, the host had also come to the end of his rope. *Donald Duck, a terrifying character? My butt!* he thought, tossing his notes aside. "Let's go to a commercial," he said to the camera.

The boys kept their laughter to themselves.

The two limousines from WKEU and WJRT entered the narrow streets of New Orleans's famous French Quarter from opposite directions, but they arrived at the same time outside the Pepper Tree Inn. The little hotel had entertained its first guests in the mid-1800s and now served as the temporary home for the cast and crew of *A Tale of Poe.* The French Quarter was quiet this

early in the morning, its sidewalks empty except for Aunt Judith and Uncle Jack, who stood waiting for their nephews outside the hotel with their arms folded tightly across their chests.

Naturally, they had tuned in to the simultaneous TV interviews—Aunt Judith watching WKEU in their hotel room, Uncle Jack watching WJRT in the boys' empty, adjacent room. Each had thought it was pure gibberish.

This was not the first time the twins had tested Uncle Jack and Aunt Judith's patience.

Edgar climbed out of one limousine.

Allan climbed out of the other.

The limos pulled away in opposite directions.

"Well, what do you boys have to say?" Uncle Jack asked sternly.

The boys looked at each other, then turned to their uncle. "Good morning?" they offered sheepishly.

Uncle Jack shook his head. "You think that's what I want to hear?"

"Well," Edgar answered, drawing patterns on the side-walk with the tip of one shoe. "It's a little early in the day to say 'good afternoon,' don't you think, Uncle Jack?"

"Yeah," Allan added, shielding his eyes from the rising

sunlight. "And saying 'good night' at this hour would be downright crazy!"

"And even though we're in New Orleans, saying '*bonjour*' seems a little pretentious," Edgar finished.

Aunt Judith rubbed her temples with the tips of her fingers, as if she had a headache. She sighed. "Where were your minds this morning?" she asked.

Their minds had been in one another's heads. As usual.

But Edgar and Allan knew that wouldn't do for an answer.

Uncle Jack and Aunt Judith didn't understand how it worked with their nephews, though they'd raised them since Edgar and Allan were orphaned at age five. The boys' parents, rocket scientists Mal and Irma Poe, had been accidentally launched into space while making final adjustments to the payload section of an Atlas V rocket. The tragedy made national news. In the ensuing seven years, Uncle Jack and Aunt Judith had loved and cared for the boys, though they never grasped just how connected their nephews were.

So, in answer to their aunt and uncle's questioning looks on the sidewalk outside the Pepper Tree Inn, the twins simply shrugged their shoulders and said, as one,

"Maybe we could have done with a little more sleep."

Just then, the international award-winning movie director Werner Wender and his assistant, Cassie Kilmer, emerged from the lobby. Cassie had been hired just a few days before. She was model-pretty. Nonetheless, Mr. Wender was, as always, the center of attention. Wearing classy shades, a white linen suit, a weathered fedora, and brand-new-out-of-the-box sneakers, he jumped down the last three stairs, landing on the sidewalk as lightly as a man half his age.

"Amazing!" he said to the Poe family. Uncle Jack and Aunt Judith looked confused.

"How'd you do it?" Mr. Wender asked the twins.

"Do what?" they inquired, putting on their most innocent expressions.

"Your TV appearances!" Cassie answered, gesturing enthusiastically. Her many bangles and charm bracelets made an unmusical clatter.

"Truly original!" Mr. Wender said, clapping the boys on their shoulders. He was unpredictable—one minute blissful, the next blue. The twins were glad that this morning he was feeling blissful.

"Someone's already posted the two interviews on the Internet, lined up side by side," Cassie explained.

"I just got the link," Mr. Wender continued. "It's creating a lot of interest in the two of you. And in our movie! And that's never a bad thing for the box office."

Uncle Jack's and Aunt Judith's eyes widened at Mr. Wender's mention of the Internet, which they considered to be darker and more dangerous than the Spanish Inquisition.

"It was as if you were each in two places at once!" Mr. Wender continued. "How'd you pull it off? Hidden microphones and earpieces?"

"Pull what off?" Aunt Judith inquired, turning to the twins.

Uncle Jack scratched his balding head.

A limousine, shinier and longer than either of the limos that had carried the boys to and from the TV studios, glided up to the curb. A uniformed driver jumped out and ran to open the back door.

"We have to go to the production office," Mr. Wender announced. "Why don't you explain your stunt to your aunt and uncle? It'll give them a good laugh. And keep up the good work, you two."

"See you this evening, boys," Cassie called.

She and Mr. Wender climbed into the limo, and the chauffeur closed the door.

And *whoosh!*

Gone.

It was a lot for Uncle Jack and Aunt Judith to take in.

Two weeks before, their nephews were fighting crime. Now it was TV, movie, and Internet stardom. . . .

"All this and it's not even eight o'clock in the morning yet," Aunt Judith observed.

Uncle Jack shrugged, as if giving up trying to understand what his nephews had gotten into this time. "Listen boys, they've got pastries here in New Orleans called beignets. They're like doughnuts, only better." He lowered his voice, turning away from Aunt Judith who didn't like him to eat sweets. "Who's up for breakfast?"

WHAT THE POE TWINS DID NOT KNOW . . .

A LETTER DATED ONE WEEK BEFORE:

Mrs. Natasha Perry
Prisoner #89372
State Prison for Women
Senior Citizen Wing
Ossining, NY 10562

Ms. Cassandra Perry
P.O. Box 3273
New Orleans, LA 70116

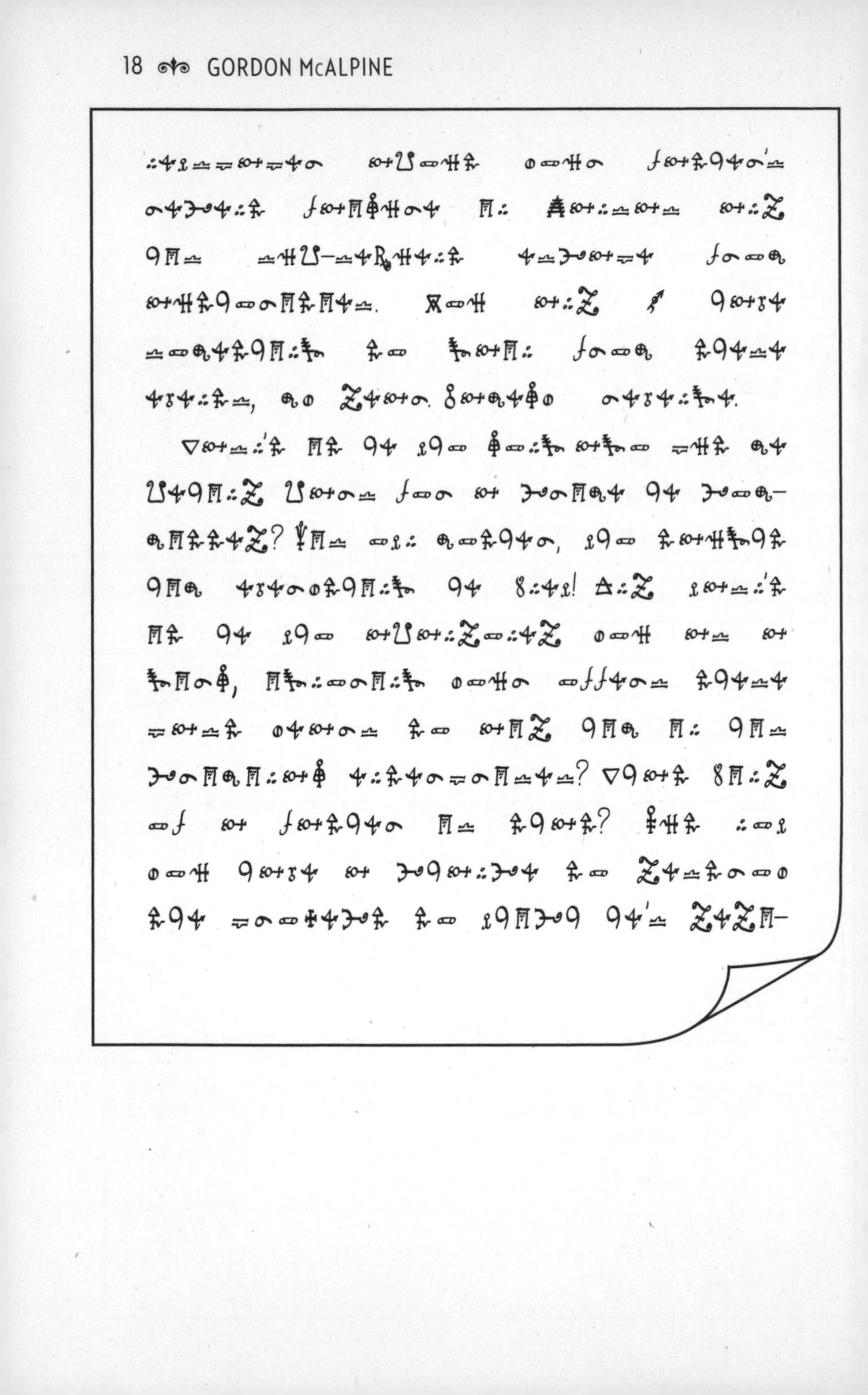

NOTE: The text of the preceding letter is written in a replacement code intended to disguise the communication as mere gibberish to prison guards or any other reader except its intended recipient. The decoded translation is as follows:

Dear Cassandra,

As your grandmother, I'm proud that you've become one of the most accomplished con artists in the entire southern United States. Your violent streak is a credit to the family. And now you've been presented with an opportunity to put your talents to great personal use!

Surely you've read in the newspaper about your father's recent failure in Kansas and his subsequent escape from authorities. You and I have something to gain from these events, my dear. Namely, revenge.

Wasn't it he who long ago put me behind bars for a crime he committed? His own mother, who taught him everything he knew! And wasn't it he who abandoned you as a girl, ignoring your offers these past years to aid him in his criminal enterprises? What kind of a father is that? But now you have a chance to destroy the project to which he's dedicated himself for more than a decade, his Edgar and Allan Poe quantum physics experiment. It is simple. All you need do is kill both of the twins before he finds a way back to this country. That'll teach him to underestimate you, my dear!

Can it be coincidence that the Poe twins are coming to New Orleans, your home? No, it is fate! I trust you can find a way to get hired onto that movie crew. You must act now. Time is short.

Grandmother

"THE STUFFED CAT"

WITH the boys' first scene not scheduled to start shooting until seven p.m., the Poe family bought tickets for a late morning tour of New Orleans on a red double-decker bus that would have looked more at home in London.

"That's strange," Allan said. "Look at the license plate."

"Seems more appropriate for a fire truck or police car than a tour bus," Edgar observed.

Allan nodded. "Unless it's not meant for everybody."

"Yeah, another warning for us."

It wasn't the first.

Since crossing into Louisiana, the boys had noticed license plates on passing cars that read:

They had kept an eye out for unusual occurrences. Still, nothing bad had happened.

At least not yet.

"Everybody on board," called the driver.

The twins left Aunt Judith and Uncle Jack on the lower level and took seats on top in the open air. On an empty seat between them, they unzipped their backpack.

Out popped the curious head of their beloved black cat, Roderick Usher.

"Hey, you can't have a cat up here," said the driver when he came to check on the upstairs guests before embarking on the tour. "This is a bus, not a circus train!"

Edgar and Allan not only disliked what the driver had to say, but also the way he said it.

He stared the boys down, his hands on his hips. "No pets allowed."

"That's cold as ice," Edgar said. *"Downright frozen."*

The driver waved his hand in front of his face as if to disperse a bad smell. "I just want that pet off my bus. Now."

The twins weren't going to leave Roderick alone all day in the hotel room.

"This isn't a pet," Allan said.

"I don't care what you call it," the driver snapped. "It's a cat."

"No, it's not," Edgar insisted.

"You think I'm blind?"

The boys shook their heads. "It used to be a cat, but it's not anymore."

Their parents had brought Roderick home as a kitten just one week before the rocket launch that took their lives. Naturally, Allan and Edgar would have loved him even if he'd been ordinary. But Roderick was not ordinary. With a figure eight of white fur against the pure black of his chest, he was very stylish. And he happened to be among the smartest cats in the world.

"He used to be a live cat," Allan explained to the driver. "But now he's more like a stuffed toy."

"Yeah, don't you recognize expert taxidermy when you see it?" asked Edgar.

The driver narrowed his eyes.

Edgar and Allan had taught Roderick many tricks. Just two weeks before, in Kansas, Roderick had saved their lives by unknotting a rope on command (the cue being the twins whistling "Ring Around the Rosy"). Additionally, Roderick could imitate the sound of a monkey whenever his masters said the words "tree swinger," the barking of a dog whenever they said "poochie," and the crying of a baby whenever they said "spilled milk." But his greatest feat was what the boys called "The Stuffed Cat"—Roderick would tighten his muscles and freeze, glassing over his eyeballs, for up to three minutes or until the boys released him with a snap of their fingers. His cue was the phrase "downright frozen."

So this was what Roderick was doing now.

"You mean taxidermy as in *dead*?" the driver asked, looking at Roderick's motionless head and eyes. "Like the stuffed animals in the natural history museum? Or a hunting lodge?"

Allan nodded. "'Taxidermy,' an early nineteenth-century word, derived from the Greek—"

"*Taxis* meaning 'arrangement,' and *derma* meaning 'skin,'" Edgar finished.

By now, a trio of female tourists, all wearing matching shirts and too much perfume, had gathered around the twins.

Edgar removed the stiff, motionless cat from the backpack and held it toward the driver. "Want to hold him?"

The man stepped back.

"My, he looks so real," said one of the ladies.

"We're *very* good taxidermists," Edgar said.

The driver took a deep breath. "Well, I guess a stuffed cat can stay."

"Thanks, sir."

Grunting, the man turned and clambered down the spiral staircase. A few moments later, the bus lurched to a start, veering into the traffic outside the tourist office.

The Poe twins turned to the trio atop the bus and winked. "Watch this, ladies," they said, snapping their fingers.

Roderick suddenly came back to life, meowing and purring.

The women jumped, startled.

Then they started laughing. "Nice trick, boys!"

"Hey, it's Roderick you should be complimenting," Allan said.

Settled in their seats, with Roderick curled between them, the twins soaked up the November sun as the bus pulled away from Jackson Square. It was warmer here than in Baltimore, where their friends would be bundled now in winter coats and mittens.

Allan and Edgar wore T-shirts.

Nothing beat a winter day spent in the warm sun, except maybe a school day spent out of school.

This was both.

It had been almost six weeks since Edgar and Allan were expelled from Aldrin Middle School, victims of Professor Perry's lies. Since then, they had not only traveled to Kansas, rescued their cat, and escaped the professor's plan for their destruction, but, in doing so, had also earned a handwritten letter from the Baltimore superintendent of schools inviting them to return to class. Of course, in the meantime, Mr. Wender had asked them to be movie actors.

So school had to wait.

They didn't miss the homework or the tests, which for Edgar and Allan were always too easy to be of much interest.

But they missed their friends.

So when the red double-decker bus drove past the magnificent old mansions on St. Charles Avenue, they thought of Katie Justus. She wanted to be an architect and spent most of her free time drawing pictures of houses with stately columns and century-old ivy, just like these.

And when the bus stopped on Magazine Street so that everyone could disembark for a lunch of po' boy sandwiches (a famous New Orleans specialty consisting of roast beef or fried oysters or shrimp on a toasted French roll), the boys wished their best friend Stevie "The Hulk" Harrison was there too. He'd probably eat three or four, if given the chance. And they regarded the sandwiches as the best-named food ever, in any language: po' boys!

"There should be an 'Edgar' and an 'Allan' variety," Edgar observed.

"Yeah, and they'd look and taste exactly alike!" said Allan.

"Bay shrimp, sauerkraut, blue cheese, and jalapeños!"

And when they stopped at the New Orleans Pirate Museum, they were reminded of their friend David Litke. He loved pirates and would have been impressed by the life-size wax figures of the notorious brothers Jean and Pierre Lafitte, who had gained pardons from the United

States president for helping to defeat the British navy in the early 1800s.

Pirates turned heroes—*that* didn't happen very often.

"Maybe we should become pirates," Edgar whispered to his brother as they lingered over a glass display case of crossed swords and authentic pirate flags.

"Good idea," Allan said. "Except . . . our days are already pretty full being archaeologists, cryptologists, linguists, detectives, and cultural critics."

They drifted toward a display case containing three gold coins, authentic Spanish doubloons. Above the case was a sign that read:

THE LAFITTE BROTHERS' HIDDEN TREASURE
HAS NEVER BEEN FOUND

"Let's go, everyone—time to move on!" called the tour guide.

For Edgar and Allan, the highlight of the tour came when the bus stopped outside the walled, centuries-old Saint Louis Cemetery, which boasted no grassy, parklike setting but instead consisted of row upon row of tightly packed, ornate, aboveground crypts. Crumbling stone angels and gargoyles watched over this chilling city of the dead.

"Let's all stay together as we walk through the

cemetery," the guide announced as the group disembarked from the bus and started toward the ornate iron gates of the necropolis. "We wouldn't want to lose any of you to local ghosts!"

Most of the group laughed, but Uncle Jack and Aunt Judith exchanged a look of anxiety.

They didn't even like spooky movies.

So real cemeteries? Forget it.

With Roderick safely tucked inside Edgar's backpack, the twins moved with the group up one avenue of macabre mausoleums and down another.

"Because of the damp conditions of the ground here in New Orleans, as well as the traditional burial practices of city founders, our cemeteries generally consist of these aboveground vaults," the guide explained.

"Creepy," murmured Aunt Judith, drifting nervously toward Uncle Jack.

Uncle Jack jumped, startled, when she unexpectedly brushed against him. "Yeah, creepy," he agreed, taking her hand.

Edgar and Allan walked behind them, smiling.

They loved the place.

And then they saw something that made them love it even more.

In the oldest section of the cemetery, many of the names and dates cut into the stone mausoleums had been worn away by two centuries of wind, rain, and sun. Generally, these markers were evenly worn. But Edgar and Allan noticed one crypt that was different. It featured a marker upon which some letters had been worn away in the ordinary fashion, while the remaining letters showed no wear *at all*.

This was the sort of thing most people didn't notice.

But Allan and Edgar had a gift for recognizing patterns where others saw only randomness. (Two connected brains were not merely twice as efficient as one, but many times more efficient.) They'd learned from license plates, fortune cookies, misprinted books and magazines, and countless other sources that the world was full of hidden messages for those willing to fully engage their perceptiveness and imagination.

They studied the two markers.

MADAME ENEVIEVE DU VALIER
ERE LIES UR ISTER
BELOVED WIFE
MAY SHE RES IN PEACE WI H R
LO D FOREVER
DIED OCTOBER FIRST, 1814
ONSI UR CLAR NCE DU VALIER
HERE LIES OUR BRO HER
BELOVED HU BAND
MAY ST IN ERC FUL AN
HO ORABLY R TEOUS SLUMBER
DIED OC OBER FIRST, 1814

A missing "G" in Genevieve, "H" in here, "O" in our, "S" in "sister," and "T" in "rest."

G-H-O-S-T . . .

Then a missing "T" in "with," "O" and "U" in "our" and "R" in "lord."

The twins examined the inscription for Genevieve's husband, Clarence, noting the order of missing letters on his marker.

Put together with those of his wife, the omissions spelled this:

GHOST TOUR MEETS HERE MIDNIGHT

WHAT THE POE TWINS DID NOT KNOW . . .

A REPLY TO GRANDMOTHER'S LETTER:

CASSANDRA PERRY

Mrs. Natasha Perry
Prisoner #89372
State Prison for Women
Senior Citizen Wing
Ossining, NY 10562

Dear Grandmother,

I received your letter. Best idea ever!

I had tea with Mr. Wender's assistant. Or should I say former assistant? Now I'm the new hire.

Yours, C

IN A KINGDOM BY THE SEA

THE Poe twins sat in their dressing room, a converted RV parked on a French Quarter street, working a French crossword puzzle to honor the founding spirit and language of New Orleans. 3 across: "What daisies use to propel a bicycle." *Pétales de fleurs*—flower petals. 11 down: "Has a head and tail but no body." *Pièce de monnaie*—a coin. The boys put down their puzzle when Mr. Wender's assistant, Cassie, strode into the trailer with a clipboard in her hand and a worried expression on her face.

"Boys, you're due on set!" she shouted, her bracelets clattering. "Do you hear me?"

The dead could probably have heard her.

"There's no cause for panic," Allan said, spying her worried face in the mirror.

"Moviemaking is nothing *but* panic!" she answered emphatically.

Ordinarily, the twins would object to being hurried. They would have found a way to turn the tables on Cassie (such as setting her watch back, or changing the time zone on her smartphone). But today they chose to cut her some slack. After all, she was new on the job and probably just wanted to impress Mr. Wender, whose previous assistant, now hospitalized, had somehow ingested a small quantity of rat poison.

And it was, after all, their first day of shooting.

"Have you learned your lines?" Cassie asked anxiously.

The twins nodded, having rehearsed the night before with Mr. Wender. A "run-through" he'd called it (previously, Edgar and Allan had thought the phrase "run through" referred only to what pirates did to others with their swords).

"Then let's go!"

Outside, the street swarmed with extras dressed in early nineteenth-century costumes, technicians, caterers, photographers, a few journalists, and a handful of production assistants who carried either clipboards (like Cassie) or cardboard trays balancing large cups of coffee.

"Hurry, hurry," Cassie implored.

In the movie, this block of New Orleans would stand in for nineteenth-century Richmond, Virginia, which had been the boyhood home of Edgar Allan Poe. The two-hundred-year-old buildings had been renovated to look new. Even the wrought iron on the balconies glistened. Expert lighting cast some sections of the set in shadow and others in a glow as mysterious as moonlight. And a camera atop a tall crane would provide a dramatic overhead view.

The twins were impressed.

"We've no time to lose." Cassie pulled the boys along, Roderick trotting behind.

"Is the set on fire or something?" Allan murmured.

"Hello, boys!" called Aunt Judith from across the set, near the buffet table. "Love your costumes!"

Uncle Jack stood beside her, talking in a loud voice about his love of old silent movies to a note-taking journalist who expressed gracious interest.

The twins started toward them to say hello, but Cassie put her perfectly manicured hands on their shoulders and steered them in the opposite direction.

"You'll have time for family later. It's moviemaking time now."

In tonight's scene, which would open the film, one of the twins would portray the author as a solitary boy meeting an entrancing twelve-year-old girl named Annabel Lee. Later in the movie, her character would prove the inspiration for one of the adult Poe's most famous poems.

> It was many and many a year ago,
> In a kingdom by the sea,
> That a maiden there lived whom you may know,
> By the name of Annabel Lee . . .

The second and final of the boys' scenes, to be shot the next day, would depict a dream in which the young Edgar Allan Poe meets his double—a good Poe/bad Poe confrontation. It would be the last scene in the movie. Originally, Mr. Wender had planned to use special effects to make one young actor appear to be two.

But then he saw Edgar and Allan on the evening news.

"Over there," Cassie said, pointing to three canvas folding chairs with names stenciled on the backs—EDGAR POE, ALLAN POE, and (best of all) RODERICK USHER. "Hurry up and sit."

Allan turned to her. "You rushed us here just so we could sit and wait?"

"Welcome to moviemaking, boys," she answered blithely, before disappearing into the crowd near the buffet table.

Reluctantly, the twins sat.

"This movie star stuff isn't as glamorous as people think," Allan observed.

Roderick meowed in sympathy as he hopped onto his chair.

From someplace behind them, a girl's voice responded to their comments.

"You two are lucky."

The boys turned.

Sitting in similar folding chairs were twin girls of about the same age as Edgar and Allan. They wore identical black nineteenth-century-style dresses, and their auburn hair was long and loose. Their eyes were luminous, and their heart-shaped faces pretty, even if their attire seemed more suitable for a funeral.

"Are you talking to us?" the boys asked.

One of the girls nodded.

Edgar and Allan noted only the slightest difference in their appearances: in the blue irises of one were tiny specks of green that were absent in the pure blue eyes of the other.

"Why do you say we're lucky?" Edgar inquired.

"Because she hurried *us* out here twenty minutes ago," said the girls.

"Are you two playing Annabel Lee?"

The girls nodded.

Edgar and Allan were not surprised to meet another set of twins here. Film companies often cast twins to play a single juvenile role, switching between them on long working days. The girls had already appeared in five scenes with the adult Poe character, "haunting" him. This was their only scene with the Poe twins.

"Of course, our real names aren't Annabel Lee," said the girl with the green in her eyes. "My real name is Em."

Em as in emerald, like the flecks in her irises—an easy way for the boys to remember which girl was which.

"And I'm Milly," said the other.

"We're Edgar and Allan Poe," they said in unison.

"Oh, we know who you are," Milly answered. She displayed a smartphone. "We've seen your pictures and followed your story on all the news sites. That is, *I* followed it." She nodded toward her sister. "Em doesn't go online."

Em shrugged off the comment. "I'm more interested

in the eternal than in that which is merely current," she said. "In short, poetry. But I *was* impressed with your valorous deeds."

"Yeah, after I told you about them," Milly said. "Otherwise, you'd never have known."

Em straightened in her chair and recited:

"Perhaps the kingdom of Heaven's changed!
I hope the children there
Won't be new-fashioned when I come,
And laugh at me, and stare!"

"See what I mean?" Milly said to the boys, shaking her head.

Edgar met Em's eyes. "That poem's by Emily Dickinson."

She nodded and smiled.

"Who else would it be by?" Milly asked. "We're the Dickinson sisters."

"Em and Milly Dickinson . . ." Allan mused aloud.

"Emily Dickinson was our great-great-great-great grandaunt," Em said proudly.

"That's amazing," said Allan. "Since our great-great-great-great grandunde—"

"Oh, we know!" Milly interrupted.

"But we don't consider our meeting you to be a coincidence," Em said. "See, we don't believe in coincidence."

The boys looked at each other—they didn't believe in coincidence either.

"We believe in fate," Em continued.

Edgar and Allan were impressed.

"Which of you is Edgar and which is Allan?" Milly asked.

Not an easy question . . .

"You can call me Allan, if you want," one of the twins volunteered, for simplicity's sake.

"And you can call me Edgar."

The girls looked relieved. Then a wave of dismay crossed Milly's face. "OK, but when you're dressed in identical costumes, like now, how can we tell you apart?"

The twins didn't have an immediate answer.

"Just call us whichever you want," Edgar said, at last.

The girls looked at each other quizzically. Then they turned to Edgar and Allan.

"You're no ordinary boys, are you," Milly observed.

The boys were uncertain how to answer.

"We don't mean that in a bad way," Em assured them.

"See, we aren't much interested in 'ordinary' boys," Milly said.

Em smiled. "Just extraordinary ones."

"Well, um, I guess that's us," they answered.

Once more, Milly displayed her phone. "Can I put your contact information in here?"

"We don't have cell phones," Allan said.

"Don't tell me you're both dinosaurs like my sister, please!"

Edgar shook his head. "It's not exactly like that."

Actually, Edgar and Allan were experts when it came to electronic technologies, particularly computer hacking. A few months before, they'd knocked out the electrical grid for the entire city of Baltimore as a prank. Afterward, they were forbidden by their aunt and uncle from touching anything attached to the Internet.

"Our aunt and uncle don't allow us to go online," Allan said.

Milly shuddered. "They must be monsters!"

Edgar shook his head. "They have their reasons."

"Actors to the set!" called a voice over a bullhorn. "Places, everybody!"

Edgar took his position in the large, open entryway of the nineteenth-century townhouse that would stand in for the author's childhood home. Skillfully backlit, he was visible only in dramatic silhouette, facing out toward the street, his arms at his sides.

"Quiet on the set!"

Moments before, Allan had lost Mr. Wender's coin flip, which had sent his brother onto the set to do the scene. (Of course, there never was any real winning or losing between the Poe twins, as each could always be said to do whatever the other did, simultaneously.)

"Action!" called Mr. Wender.

YOUNG EDGAR ALLAN POE stands motionless in the doorway. Then, as if giving himself over to a strange, magnetic pull, he steps out of the townhouse and onto the sidewalk, transforming from mysterious silhouette to dimly lit figure. He takes slow steps. At last, he stops in the flickering glow of a gas streetlamp that illuminates his face, which bears an expression almost as dark as the night around him. This is no carefree boy. From out of the darkness comes a girl's voice, unexpected but appealing.

ANNABEL LEE

"Is this your cat, sir?"

EDGAR turns, spying a lovely young girl *[played by Em]* kneeling beside a black cat *[played by Roderick]*.

The scene continued as planned until Edgar delivered his last line. Then, instead of walking silently out of the shot after him, as expected, Em turned to the camera and delivered the following speech:

ANNABEL LEE

(to YOUNG EDGAR ALLAN POE)

Your wisdom is consumed in confidence.

Do not go forth to-day: call it my fear

That keeps you in the house, and not your own.

Edgar looked at her, befuddled.

"Cut!" Mr. Wender shouted, striding out from behind the monitor. "What on earth are you doing, Miss Dickinson?" he demanded, his German accent thickening as he grew angrier.

"It's the new version of the scene," Em said nervously.

"There *is* no new version," Mr. Wender snapped. "And I'd know, *since I wrote the script.*"

"But there was a page on my chair. It said 'New dialogue for scene one.'" She hurried to get it for him.

The director took it, looked it over, and then angrily crumpled it into a ball and tossed it away.

Everyone stood Stuffed Cat-still in response to his rage.

"Does anyone here have a *proper* copy of the script to show this young lady?" he demanded.

Everyone looked at their scripts.

Simultaneously, their faces registered surprise.

Somehow, the speech had been added to *all* of the copies of the script.

Impossible—but nothing piqued the boys' interest like "impossible" occurrences.

Allan went over to the director. "That speech may be a message to my brother and me."

"What?" he asked.

"Sometimes the universe sends us messages in mysterious forms."

Mr. Wender sighed. "Look, boys, this is no time for jokes."

But the boys weren't joking.

And neither was the mysteriously inserted speech.

"It's from Shakespeare's play *Julius Caesar,*" Edgar explained.

"Caesar's wife is trying to warn him that he's about to be assassinated," Allan added, glancing meaningfully at his brother.

A warning about assassination?

For Edgar and Allan, this was nothing new.

Mr. Wender waved his hands dismissively.

The Poe twins didn't dismiss the warning. But neither would they allow it to alter their immediate priority, which was to finish shooting tonight's scene with time enough to return to the Pepper Tree Inn, pretend to go to sleep, and then sneak out for the midnight ghost tour. Edgar and Allan never allowed caution to overrule curiosity.

"Quiet on the set!"

Edgar returned to his original, silhouetted position in the doorway.

After a moment, Mr. Wender called: "Action!"

Edgar and Em played the scene without the final speech.

"Cut! And print!" called Mr. Wender happily.

Three hours later, after additional takes with the camera in different positions, Mr. Wender strode to the middle of the set and raised his arms joyfully to the skies.

"That's a wrap for tonight, everyone!" he announced.

It was eleven o'clock and the ghost tour was scheduled to begin in an hour. The boys said quick good-byes to Em and Milly, who had made good first impressions (each in her own way). Roderick wove a quick figure eight around their legs. Then boys and cat raced across the set to Uncle Jack and Aunt Judith, who had spent most of the evening watching from their nephews' personalized chairs.

"Let's get back to the hotel," Edgar said to them.

"Growing boys need a decent bedtime," Allan added.

Uncle Jack and Aunt Judith looked at them suspiciously.

The boys responded with jaw-cracking yawns.

"OK," Uncle Jack said. "Bedtime it is."

Bedtime, sure, thought Edgar and Allan.

WHAT THE POE TWINS DID NOT KNOW . . .

TRANSCRIPT OF PHONE CONVERSATION RECORDED AT STATE PRISON FOR WOMEN, SENIOR CITIZEN UNIT:

FEMALE: Hello?

INMATE #89372: Hello, Cassandra?

FEMALE: Grandmother? It's after eleven. We just finished shooting. Is everything all right?

INMATE #89372: Oh yes, I have wonderful news.

FEMALE: You mean about our plan? Oh, I've already laid the groundwork.

INMATE #89372: No. Something else. But just as good. I've kept it to myself because I wasn't sure it would really happen. But it has. I've been paroled!

FEMALE: That's fantastic!

INMATE #89372: Twenty-six long years. . . . Now I can come to New Orleans.

FEMALE: To assist me?

INMATE #89372: Exactly.

Mr. Poe in the Great Beyond

Mr. Edgar Allan Poe, who had been dead now for more than one hundred and sixty years, slammed his fist on his desk, rattling his stapler, tape dispenser, coffee mug, pen and inkwell, and framed photograph of his great-great-great-great grandnephews, Edgar and Allan. His

life on earth had not been easy; likewise, his afterlife, spent working in various writing department cubicles, had offered its share of frustrations. Most recently, he had been demoted from the Fortune Cookie Division to the License Plate Division.

And now this:

See me in my office, now!

Wm. Shakespeare

That Mr. Shakespeare wanted to meet in his own office was not a good sign. He usually came to Mr. Poe's cubicle to register his displeasure with Mr. Poe's projects, particularly those involving Edgar and Allan. He used his own office for only the most serious matters.

Drat!

So Mr. Poe took the elevator to the 184,692,384th floor, roughly the middle of the building.

The first thing Mr. Poe always noticed when he entered Mr. Shakespeare's office was how thick and cushy the carpeting felt. It was almost like walking on a cloud.

Next, he took in the theatrical posters that lined the paneled walls. These changed daily, representing a selection of Mr. Shakespeare's plays currently running in theaters on earth. Almost every country was represented.

Finally, Mr. Poe noted that the curtain was drawn across the office's magnificent picture window. Ordinarily, Mr. Shakespeare took great pride in sharing the breathtaking view from this perch in the celestial skyscraper. The drawn curtain was a bad sign.

Mr. Shakespeare stood behind his big desk. "Come in, Mr. Poe."

It was only then that Mr. Poe realized they were not alone.

He gasped when he recognized the old man sitting on the oversize sofa.

It was Mr. Shakespeare's boss: Homer, the ninth-century B.C. author of *The Iliad* and *The Odyssey,* father of Western literature, and, most impressive, the writing department liaison to the executive suite upstairs.

Mr. Poe was speechless.

"Join me here on the couch, Mr. Poe," Homer said, his blind eyes seeming to have zeroed in on the suddenly humbled American poet and short story writer.

"Um, yes, sir."

Mr. Poe had met Homer only once before, at a writing department Halloween party. Homer had come costumed as a baseball player. Now, he wore a brightly colored tunic and his bearded face bore a chiseled dignity that even the finest Greek sculptor had failed to capture.

"It seems we have a problem, Mr. Poe," Mr. Shakespeare said, pulling distractedly at his doublet.

What else is new? Mr. Poe thought, sitting at the far end of the sofa.

Homer turned to him. "How are you these days, Edgar?"

"Oh, fine," he answered nervously.

Homer said nothing but merely waited, his blind gaze boring into Mr. Poe.

"OK—actually, I'm not fine but worried, sir," Mr. Poe said. "See, my nephews on earth are in great danger." He leaned across the couch and gestured dramatically, even though Homer could not see. "Please understand, they're extraordinary boys and—"

Homer held up one large, wizened hand.

Mr. Poe stopped.

Mr. Shakespeare sat on the edge of his desk. "Rest assured, Mr. Poe, that Homer knows all about your nephews. And, more significantly, he also knows about your recent efforts to intervene—or shall I say, *interfere*—with their lives on earth, including your recent license plate warnings."

Yes, Mr. Poe had been quite busy of late breaking rules.

"But plagiarism is a whole other level of offense," Homer interjected calmly.

In the presence of the Greek master, Mr. Poe hadn't the will to make the sort of sarcastic remarks that he usually directed toward Mr. Shakespeare. Instead, he just looked away.

"Of course, we refer to your most recent warning to the boys," Mr. Shakespeare added, anger edging into his voice. "Specifically, the alterations to the movie script being filmed now in New Orleans."

Mr. Poe gave him a deliberately blank look. "Movie?"

"I'm afraid this time you've gone too far," said Homer.

"Have you ever considered, sir, that perhaps someone

else might have sent a warning down to my nephews?" He glanced at Mr. Shakespeare. "Even my boss here, for example."

Mr. Shakespeare laughed maliciously.

"Yes, we considered that, Mr. Poe," Homer said. "That's precisely the trouble."

Mr. Poe tried to look surprised by the accusation. But he feared he'd never fool Homer, whose insight was not reliant on his eyes alone.

Homer recited from memory:

> "Your wisdom is consumed in confidence
> Do not go forth to-day: call it my fear
> That keeps you in the house, and not your own."

Mr. Shakespeare stood up and glared at Mr. Poe. "Those lines are taken word for word from *my* play *Julius Caesar*, act two, scene two!"

Mr. Poe said nothing.

"Somehow, you used my log-in to access the Dramatists' Archives. This flies in the face of all rules, Mr. Poe. Especially since you'd been assigned to the License Plate Division!"

"Temper your temper, Will," Homer said.

Mr. Shakespeare nodded, closed his eyes, and took a deep, calming breath.

When he spoke again, his manner was as composed as a prosecutor's in a courtroom. "What matters is that Mr. Poe communicated a warning to his nephews by appropriating *my* words, thereby attempting to place the blame for the malfeasance on me. To say nothing of plagiarism. . . . This, I dare say, is an offense of great seriousness."

"I am no plagiarist, dear sir!" Mr. Poe fired back.

"Yet you stole my words."

"Perhaps I used them. But I never claimed them as my own." Then Mr. Poe grinned. "Nor would I *want* to."

"That's enough between you two," Homer said.

Mr. Shakespeare turned imperiously to Mr. Poe. "You may return to your cubicle now. Homer and I will discuss appropriate disciplinary action."

Mr. Poe turned to go. He wasn't too worried.

They'd already busted him down to the License Plate Division.

How much lower could it go?

'ROUND MIDNIGHT

AT twenty minutes to midnight, Edgar and Allan said good night to Aunt Judith and Uncle Jack in the cozy, antique-rich lobby of the Pepper Tree Inn.

Aunt Judith kissed each boy on his cheek.

"'Night, gentlemen," Uncle Jack said, patting their heads.

Edgar and Allan started for the stairway, Roderick trotting at their heels.

But at the foot of the stairs, the trio stopped and turned back.

"Aren't you coming up, too?" Allan asked.

Uncle Jack shook his head "We thought we'd sit in the lobby for a little while."

"Maybe have a cup of chamomile tea," Aunt Judith added.

The boys looked at each other.

Uncle Jack and Aunt Judith would never allow them to go outside after midnight. So how were they to sneak out in time to make the Midnight Ghost Tour, which was scheduled to start in just twenty minutes?

"You boys look worried," Uncle Jack observed.

"We are," Allan said. "About you two."

"Us?" Uncle Jack asked, glancing at his wife. "Why?"

"It's been a long day, and you two should get to bed. Sipping tea all night is reckless, dangerous behavior. Even chamomile."

Aunt Judith raised her eyebrows.

"What we're saying," added Edgar, "is that we've all had a long day. And just as young people need sleep, so do old people."

This didn't go over very well.

"Hey!" Aunt Judith snapped. "We're not *old*."

"Yeah, we're middle-aged at most," Uncle Jack said.

"But you're correct, boys, about *young* people needing their sleep," Aunt Judith said, motioning the two upstairs. "Now, nighty-night."

The twins sighed. "Okay, good night," they said, and turned and started up the stairs.

Once in their third-floor room, the twins took stock

of their options. The first was to postpone their visit to the cemetery until tomorrow night, when their aunt and uncle might go to bed earlier. The other was to climb out the window and onto the narrow brick ledge that wrapped around the outside of the building, and crawl on hands and knees to the far corner of the hotel, where they could shin down the side of a wrought-iron balcony to an alley below.

"Which option do you like, Roderick?" Allan asked.

Roderick turned his head toward the window.

"Let's go," Edgar said.

Roderick led the way, being not only the most surefooted but also the most instinctive aerial pathfinder.

Edgar and Allan followed cautiously. "Don't look down, Roderick," Allan called ahead.

Striding casually along the ledge, Roderick glanced back at the twins with an insulted expression, reminding them that no self-respecting cat had ever suffered from fear of heights.

The same could not be said of self-respecting boys.

Being three stories up seemed much higher as they crawled on the narrow ledge than it did when they just took in the view from a window. And, as they soon discovered, sections of the old ledge were crumbling. They inched across the building's facade, Allan looking ahead at Roderick's tail, Edgar looking ahead at the soles of Allan's shoes. Neither boy dared glance down.

A piece of the ledge came away as they neared the balcony.

Allan and Edgar heard the brick crash three stories below.

The boys froze, hoping no one would look up.

Meanwhile, Roderick leaped neatly onto the wrought iron and waited.

"If Roderick can do it . . ." Edgar muttered.

Allan reached across the empty space and grasped the wrought iron, sighing in relief.

He started shinning down the balcony.

Edgar followed.

"We could use stunt doubles," he remarked as they neared the ground.

"Where's the fun in that?" Allan replied.

Soon they were on solid ground in the alley outside the Pepper Tree Inn.

"Hi, boys," said Em and Milly Dickinson, who stood on the sidewalk, arms crossed.

Milly wore jeans, a T-shirt, and a light jacket. But Em looked as if she was still in costume, in a white, floor-length dress with a collar that reached almost to her chin. Her hair was pulled back into a bun. The boys noted how much she looked like the famous photograph of her great-great-great-great grandaunt.

"What are *you* two doing here?" Edgar asked.

Em pointed up to the third-floor ledge, and then across to the window from which the Poe twins had emerged. "You crawled right past our window, so we came downstairs to meet you."

"Are you sneaking out to go to a jazz club?" Milly asked. "It's New Orleans, after all."

Edgar and Allan looked at each other but said nothing.

"You didn't expect us to just let you two have all the fun, did you?"

"How'd you get down here?" Allan asked.

"The stairs," Em said.

"But weren't our aunt and uncle in the lobby, sipping tea?"

"We told them we were going out for fresh air," Milly said.

Em added, "Actually, what I told them was 'My cocoon tightens, colors tease, I'm feeling for the air.'"

Milly rolled her eyes and turned back to the boys. "Anyway, your aunt and uncle just told us not to wander far and then let us go outside. After all, they're not *our* guardians."

"You didn't say anything about our—" Edgar began.

"Don't worry," she said, "we didn't tell them about your little Spider-Man stunt on the window ledge, which, incidentally, I got on my phone. Maybe I'll post it to my blog, as one of the 'inside features' on the making of our movie."

"And *your* parents?" Allan asked.

"Oh, they're sleeping peacefully, so we needn't worry about them," Em said.

"OK, fine, you can come with us. But we don't have time for chitchat."

"It's almost midnight," Allan added.

"What, are you turning into pumpkins or something?" Em asked.

"We have an appointment."

"Where are we going?" Milly held up her phone. "I can Google the most direct route."

The boys already knew where they were going.

"Look, if you two are fast enough runners, you're welcome to come along," Allan said.

Then the boys took off.

The girls kept up just fine.

It was three minutes to midnight when the Poe and Dickinson twins arrived at the gates of Saint Louis Cemetery, panting from their run. They'd pushed through the throngs of tourists on Bourbon Street, turned up Toulouse, and continued past Rampart, all the time with Roderick clinging to the back of Allan's shirt like a feline backpack.

At the cemetery, they caught their breath.

Looking around, they were surprised how quickly the neighborhood had turned from boisterousness to stillness and solitude. Here it seemed as if they were miles from the bright lights, jazz music, and tourists, instead of just a few blocks away.

Naturally, Em had something to say:

"Great streets of silence led away
To neighborhoods of pause;
Here was no notice, no dissent,
No universe, no laws. . . ."

The front gate of the cemetery was locked.

This might have been a problem were it not for the crumbling condition of the cemetery walls.

In no time, the four found a crevice.

They climbed through just as a bell chimed midnight.

"We made it!" the boys said.

On the run here, they had explained to Em and Milly where they were going, and why.

But inside the cemetery grounds all was still.

"Hello?" called Edgar into the night.

"We've come for the tour," Allan added, his voice

echoing off the crumbling stone mausoleums. "Anybody here?"

No answer.

The four moved deeper into the cemetery, continuing up one row of gravesites and down the next.

"Is it possible you two might have misunderstood those worn-away letters?" Em asked.

As if in answer, a shadowy figure emerged from around one of the mausoleums. He spoke with a French accent. "Did you say you're here for the tour?"

A man stepped into the moonlight. He wore a tall hat, an old-fashioned cutaway coat with long tails, a frilly linen shirt, and a cravat. His sideburns were long and reached halfway across his cheeks. In short, he sported an early nineteenth-century style, like old pictures of President Andrew Jackson. *"Bonsoir, mes petits,"* he said. "Welcome."

His voice was reassuring.

A second shadow emerged, this time revealing itself as a woman, likewise dressed in the fashion of the Regency period—a long dress with a high waistline and a small but elaborate bonnet atop her head. "So glad you could join us," she said, her voice almost musical.

"You're the guides for the ghost tour?" Edgar asked the man.

"Yes, I'm Clarence Du Valier." He bowed. "And this is my wife."

"Genevieve," she said, curtsying.

The boys thought it clever that the tour guides used the names of the long-deceased New Orleans residents whose weathered stones had served as "advertisements."

"Are there others here tonight for the tour?" Allan asked.

The man shook his head. "Our means of publicizing our enterprise is very selective."

"The missing letters on the grave markers," said Milly. "Not exactly a Super Bowl commercial."

Clarence turned to her, frowning. "What is a 'super bowl'?"

"Or a 'commercial'?" Genevieve asked.

The four children looked askance at them.

Then the Poes realized that the pair must be portraying period characters to add authenticity to the tour—like hired actors at Disneyland who pretend to be Sleeping Beauty or Peter Pan, or "residents" of a living history museum. It was only natural that they'd claim not to know what a Super Bowl commercial was.

"Oh, we might have chosen another method by which to advertise our endeavor," Clarence said. "We could have employed an ordinary wooden sign, for example, of the sort you find hanging outside pubs or shoemakers' shops."

Allan played along. "Or blacksmiths'."

Clarence nodded, his expression still serious. "Exactly. But we opted for subtlety, so as to attract only a *very* clever clientele."

"And you're it, children!" Genevieve added, beaming.

"Our first customers!" Clarence said.

"Have you been at this long?" Allan asked.

Clarence and Genevieve looked at each other tenderly. Then they turned back to the Poes and Dickinsons. "Yes, a long time."

"Maybe we should get started," Allan suggested.

"*Oui*, let's go," Genevieve said, leading the way.

"Wait, can you two stand still for a minute so I can get your picture before we start?" Milly asked.

The tour guides looked at her, confused.

"You want to draw our picture?" Clarence asked.

"Won't that take quite a while?" Genevieve added.

Milly didn't bother answering. She aimed her phone, snapped—*flash!*—and then looked at the screen, baffled.

"Weird. It's not working. Nobody's in the picture."

"Let's just go!" cried Edgar and Allan.

Roderick meowed.

Cat at their side, the two sets of twins followed Clarence and Genevieve down a long row of aboveground tombs. The boys expected the costumed guides to stop at any moment, since it seemed unlikely any place could be more haunted than a cemetery. But the Du Valiers continued silently to an open auxiliary gate in the wall of the cemetery and then strode out onto Basin Street.

"Where's our first stop?" Allan asked.

"We will begin just up the street," Clarence said.

The four had to scramble to keep up, as the Du Valiers set a surprising pace. For older folks, their movements were graceful and effortless.

"This is our first site," Genevieve announced, stopping on the sidewalk before an empty lot that was overgrown with weeds and littered with broken bottles and wadded-up fast-food bags.

The twins joined the tour guides. "Here? This?"

Clarence motioned at the abandoned lot with a sweep of his hand. "You children see before you the beautiful

town house of Etienne de Boré, who became the first mayor of New Orleans in 1803."

"Yes, and you'll notice the lovely balconies and flower boxes, overflowing with our city's beloved bougainvillea," Genevieve added, gazing rapturously at the vacant lot. "Ah, Madame de Boré was such a decorous and stylish woman. And quite good on the harpsichord, too!"

The two sets of twins looked at each other. The lot was vacant. Were they missing something here?

"And if you observe above the front doorway, you'll

see an architectural flourish that's likely of particular interest to a pair of adventurous boys like you," Clarence continued, grinning widely as he pointed at empty space. "That's right—crossed muskets!"

Allan and Edgar furrowed their brows in confusion.

"You see," Clarence continued, "Monsieur de Boré had been a musketeer for the king of France before coming to the Louisiana Territory."

"Are you telling us this is where his house *used* to stand?" Em asked Clarence.

Clarence laughed. "What do you mean, 'used to'? The house is there before us!"

Ah, so this is how the tour would work, the boys surmised. They were being asked to use their imaginations.

Imagination was no problem for the Poe twins.

Em caught on too. She spoke, her voice dreamy:

"The gleam of an heroic act,
Such strange illumination—
The Possible's slow fuse is lit
By the Imagination!"

"More Dickinson," Edgar observed.

Milly groaned. "Naturally."

"Do you ever quote *our* ancestor, Mr. Edgar Allan Poe?" Allan asked Em.

She smiled at him. "'Nevermore,'"she said, quoting from Mr. Poe's best known poem, "The Raven."

The boys grinned at the acknowledgment.

"So is this Etienne a ghost?" Milly asked the guides, returning to the subject at hand.

Clarence and Genevieve turned to her with curious expressions.

"No, he died peacefully in his sleep and has moved on," Clarence said.

"Then does his wife haunt this place?" Allan inquired.

Genevieve shook her head no. "She died peacefully, too."

"So why—"

But Clarence and Genevieve had already started up the street.

"Come!" Clarence called over his shoulder.

"We've still much to see!" Genevieve added, looking back with a charming smile.

"Strange tour," Milly whispered.

The Du Valiers stopped after a few blocks at yet another vacant lot.

Sure enough, Clarence motioned to the weedy property. "Here stands the friendly pub called the Wet

Whistle, where a thirsty man can get delicious ale."

"Once, Clarence and I were proprietors of this fine establishment," Genevieve said.

Clarence turned to his wife with love in his eyes. "Yes, we had many good years, eh, dear?"

"Hey, this is supposed to be a ghost tour, right?" Allan interrupted.

"We're really not that interested in vacant lots," Edgar added. "Unless they're haunted."

Clarence turned from the lot to face the boys. "Wait a minute. . . ." He took a long, deep breath, his eyes expressing new concern. "What do you mean 'vacant lot'?"

"What else would you call this?"

"That's all you boys see here, a vacant lot?"

The Poe twins nodded.

Clarence turned to Em and Milly. "Is that all you two see?"

The girls nodded.

"Is it at least haunted?" Edgar asked.

Genevieve touched her husband gently on the shoulder, worry in her eyes. Then she turned to the four twins. "No, *it's* not haunted."

"So what's up with this tour, anyway?" Milly asked.

"We came to see haunted places," Edgar reminded him.

The man sighed. "Ah, a misunderstanding."

"What do you mean?"

"These 'vacant lots' do not appear vacant to us," Genevieve explained gently. She seemed to be sorting through the misunderstanding as she spoke. "Instead, my young friends, they're alive with what to you must seem the distant past."

"Are you speaking in metaphor?" Em asked, confused.

The Du Valiers shook their heads.

"So you actually *see* these long-gone, historical places?" asked Edgar.

"We see them because my wife and I are of the same long-gone, historical time," Clarence said.

"We thought you boys understood that," Genevieve added. Seeing the twins' baffled expressions, she continued: "This 'ghost tour' is not a tour of ghostly places, but a tour of New Orleans as we knew it, *conducted* by ghosts."

The two sets of twins stepped back as all began to comprehend.

"Our apologies," Clarence Du Valier said, removing

his head from his shoulders and cradling it in one arm, like the Headless Horseman, only real.

Em and Milly gasped.

Edgar and Allan groaned—this was *almost* too much, even for them.

Genevieve Du Valier sighed and began to grow transparent.

Edgar, Allan, Em, and Milly stood Stuffed Cat–still beside one another, their faces white as the moon overhead.

Only Roderick seemed unfazed.

"Please don't be afraid, children," Clarence said, putting his head back on his shoulders.

"We mean you no harm," Genevieve assured them, growing ever more transparent. "We mean no harm to anyone."

Shock stilled the tongues of both sets of twins.

But after a moment, Roderick sauntered toward Clarence and Genevieve, purring.

This reassured the boys.

"So, you two are . . . dead," Edgar said uncertainly.

"Well, in a manner of speaking," Clarence began, adjusting the fit of his head on his neck. "Biologically, I suppose it's undeniable." He rubbed his hands together, looking for the right words. "Physiologically, anatomically, organically, so to speak—"

"In a word, 'yes,'" Genevieve interrupted, for clarity's sake.

Edgar and Allan looked at each other in delight.

This was the best ghost tour ever!

"Is this one of your tricks?" Milly whispered to the boys.

"We've heard about you two," Em added.

The Poes shook their heads. It was true they'd pulled some ghoulish Halloween hijinks in the past, most recently turning their house into a dungeon to take revenge on neighborhood bullies. But this was the real thing.

The girls looked at each other, understanding.

"Death is a dialogue Between
The Spirit and the Dust,"

Em muttered.

This time, even Milly thought the quote perfect.

WHAT THE POE TWINS DID NOT KNOW . . .

A LETTER DELIVERED THAT DAY:

IGER COFFIN MAKERS

Serving discreet customers since 1845

Ms. Cassandra Perry

P.O. Box 3273

New Orleans, LA 70116

Dear Ms. Perry,

I received a phone call from your lovely grandmother today and she informed me that you may be interested in my services. As you know, your family is very special to me. In that light, I can make you an outstanding offer on TWO child-sized models. And I will be happy to throw in a cat-sized coffin for free.

Please let me know if I can be of any other service to you.

Markus Iger, Esq.

"WE SHALL MAKE A PIE, SIR!"

NEITHER the Poe nor the Dickinson twins were of any mind to go to sleep when they got back to the Pepper Tree Inn.

Actually, they weren't sure they'd ever sleep again.

So they crept through the silent, three a.m. lobby, careful not to wake the snoring front desk clerk, who reclined in his chair with a thick biography of George Washington Carver open on his chest. With Roderick at their heels, the four slipped up the carpeted stairway, past the third floor, to the roof, which was accessible through a heavy metal door.

They stumbled outside into the moonlight.

The view was beautiful.

To the south, the shimmering Mississippi River twisted toward the sea, and to the north the moon illuminated lacy clouds that by morning would be dew on the wrought-iron handrails and ornaments of the French Quarter. But neither Poes nor Dickinsons noted the view. Instead, they stood facing each other, their expressions similarly composed of fifty percent wonder and fifty percent dismay.

"Did we actually see what we just saw?" Milly asked the others.

"Did we just hear what we just heard?" wondered Edgar aloud.

After the Du Valiers had acknowledged their shocking condition, they invited the two sets of twins to return with them to Saint Louis Cemetery for a little socializing. There, after they had all settled on stone benches near the Du Valiers' crypt, the kindly old couple answered a flurry of questions.

Did death hurt? *Not at all.*

Did they ever get hungry? *Only for beignets, the scent of which sometimes wafted on a river breeze all the way to the cemetery.*

Why didn't they just rejoin the living, since their appearances were so lifelike? *Because they could only materialize within a mile of their tomb and only for a few hours at a time.*

What did they miss most about being alive? *The feel of one another's actual flesh when they held hands.*

What hopes did they have for the future? *To move on to the next world.*

Now, atop the roof, the Poes and Dickinsons took long, deep breaths, hoping to appear more calm and at ease than they actually were. Only Roderick seemed truly composed, curling his body into a comfortable position for a long-overdue sleep.

The four sat on the rooftop, legs crossed, as if around an invisible campfire.

"We have to talk," Allan announced.

Everyone nodded.

But where to start?

Em spoke first, or, rather, recited:

> "The grave my little cottage is,
> Where 'Keeping house' for thee,
> I make my parlor orderly
> And lay the marble tea. . . ."

"Well, one thing's for sure," Allan said, rubbing his hands to warm them, wishing that they were seated around an actual campfire rather than an imaginary one. "Clarence and Genevieve have been stuck here a long time."

Edgar reviewed aloud. "Clarence said the only way he and Genevieve could move on from this world to the next was for justice to be served."

"A public acknowledgment of their murderer's identity," Allan elaborated.

The boys thought of their parents, deceased for seven years. Surely, Mal and Irma Poe had moved on by now to the next world, having been victims of a famous accident rather than an unsolved murder. But what if circumstances had been different? Edgar and Allan shuddered to think of their mom and dad stuck, like the Du Valiers, in a cemetery (or a satellite!) for eternity. That would be unacceptable. So, in that light, how could the boys not do all they could to help Clarence and Genevieve?

"But how can we mete out justice at this late date?" Em asked, wrapping her shawl more tightly around her shoulders.

"Especially," Milly added, "since the Du Valiers' murderer has been dead for two centuries?"

"Well, obviously what we have to do is—" Allan stopped.

But Edgar didn't jump in.

The girls waited.

The Poe twins said nothing more.

"Do what?" Milly pressed after a moment.

"*That* is the question," Allan answered dramatically.

The Dickinson twins sighed and rolled their eyes.

"Great," Em said. "What we need is Sherlock Holmes, and what we get is Hamlet, prince of indecision."

The Poe twins were impressed by the literary reference, even if it was intended as a put-down.

For a while, they all sat silently on the rooftop, reviewing the facts.

This much was true:

Clarence and Genevieve Du Valier had shared all they knew of how things worked with the dead. Of course, the Du Valiers didn't know much, since they'd never moved from here to the next world. Most dead move right along; but, because the Du Valiers' double murder in 1814 had been neither solved nor avenged, they remained earthbound, pining for justice.

Naturally, they *wanted* to move on. But they needed help.

Clarence and Genevieve had explained that in the autumn of 1814, their little inn, the Wet Whistle, had been visited by the most famous brothers in all of Louisiana, the pirates Jean and Pierre Lafitte. Jean lived up to his nickname "the Gentleman Pirate." But Pierre was no gentleman at all.

Now Milly began typing on her phone.

The Poe twins had never seen anyone so adept with her thumbs.

"What are you doing?" Edgar asked.

"I'm writing a draft post for my blog," she answered, without looking up. "To take the story public!"

The Poe twins looked over her shoulder:

> One night in New Orleans, 1814, the famous Jean Lafitte left his brother Pierre and their pirate friends at the Wet Whistle. At closing time, the drunken Pierre accidentally handed the innkeeper, Clarence Du Valier, a handwritten note instead of cash. Naturally, Clarence read the note, which was just an odd-sounding poem. He returned to Pierre to explain the mistake, but the pirate leaped from his chair in outrage.
>
> "That note was for no one's eyes save my brother's and mine own!" Pierre shouted, snatching the slip of paper. "Did you read it, swine?"
>
> Clarence nodded, unable to lie.
>
> Furious, the drunken pirate

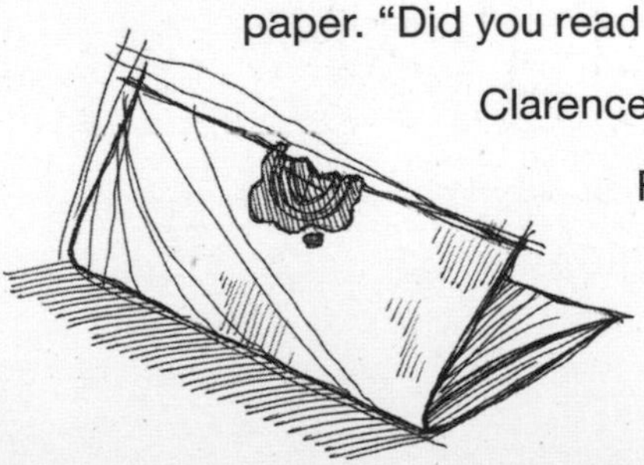

demanded that Clarence step outside to settle the matter "honorably."

In those days, that meant a duel with swords.

What Pierre Lafitte didn't know was that as a young man, Clarence had served the king of France and was an expert swordsman. In the alley behind the inn, Clarence held his own.

But it was to be no fair duel.

When Clarence's foil scratched Pierre's cheek, the pirate's henchmen grabbed the innkeeper by his arms, stripping him of his weapon. Then Pierre ran him through the heart. When Genevieve darted into the alley to help, he ran her through too.

"I will make my confession to my personal diary," Pierre declared, dropping his foil to the ground beside the dying Du Valiers. "So you two innkeepers needn't worry about my soul." Then he instructed his henchmen to behead the Du Valiers with sabers.

Pierre never answered for the crime.

Milly's thumbs stopped.

Em wiped at a tear. "Well written, sister."

"Isn't it strange," Allan commented, "that we think the Du Valiers haunt New Orleans, when it's really New Orleans that haunts them?"

"While a wax figure stands in the museum celebrating Pierre Lafitte as a hero," Edgar added.

Milly indicated the phone. "Soon it'll be online for the world to read."

"We'll still need *proof*," Em countered. "And the only proof would be Pierre's diary. His 'confession,' right?"

Milly and the Poe twins nodded.

It was commonly believed that Pierre's diary had been buried along with the Lafitte brothers' loot, which for two centuries no treasure hunter had located. However, no one had ever been provided with the clue that Clarence had offered the Poe and Dickinson twins in his account of the murder.

Now Em recited from memory the contents of Pierre's note—his poem:

"Thrice concealed in the following prose
The place where only a true Lafitte goes,
The name of the spot walled by hallowed gates

Where our treasure abides and safely awaits.

'I'll make a wise phrase.

Hear me as I will speak.

We shall make a pie, sir!'"

"It's a rather awkward poem," Em observed.

"It goes all crazy at the end," Milly added.

"I don't think the poetry is the point," Edgar said.

The girls looked at him, intrigued.

He shivered in the predawn cold. "This has something to do with the treasure."

"What else would have been so important to Pierre Lafitte that he'd kill somebody just for looking at it?" Allan added.

"So we should think about it line by line." Em stood and began to pace about the rooftop.

"'Thrice concealed in the following prose . . . '" Edgar said contemplatively.

Em turned to them, her face alight. "The 'prose' is the three unrhymed sentences at the end."

"That makes sense," Milly murmured, "but what's concealed there?"

"The name of the 'spot walled by hallowed gates,'" Edgar said.

"'Hallowed gates' . . ." Milly mused. "A cemetery!"

"And in 1814 there was only one main cemetery in New Orleans," Allan added, glad that he'd paid attention to the city tour earlier in the day. "And that cemetery is the one we visited tonight, Saint Louis Cemetery."

"So the treasure's hidden in one of the tombs?" Em said.

The Poe twins nodded.

"But which?"

The boys knew better than to quote Hamlet again and say, *That is the question.*

But that *was* the question.

And the answer was concealed three times in the three sentences at the end of the note.

> "I'll make a wise phrase.
> Hear me as I will speak.
> We shall make a pie, sir!"

"What does pie have to do with pirate treasure?" Em inquired.

"Well, what types of pie are there?" Milly asked. "Let's consider."

"I don't think that's the direction—" Allan began.

Milly dismissed him with a wave. "Off the top of my head I can think of apple, strawberry, rhubarb, chocolate, boysenberry, cherry, pumpkin, banana cream, pecan, sweet potato, coconut cream, peach, Mississippi Mud—"

The boys turned to her, their interest piqued. "Wait," Edgar said.

"Did you just say 'Mississippi Mud'?" Allan asked. They were, after all, mere walking distance to the Mississippi River, also known as "the Big Muddy." "But if the treasure's buried in the Mississippi mud . . . that's no clue at all, since the river is a thousand miles long."

Milly barely missed a beat. "Blueberry, blackberry, key lime, lemon—"

"Chess pie!" Em interrupted.

The boys turned to her.

"How's that helpful?" Edgar asked.

Em shrugged. "Well, I like to play chess in my mind whenever there's a question I can't answer."

"Why?" Allan asked.

"Chess busies my thoughts and frees them, all at the same time," she answered. "And there is, of course, a kind of pie named chess pie, of which our famous great-great-great-great grandaunt was very fond . . ."

Edgar and Allan sighed.

All the while, Milly kept reciting. "Boston cream, chicken pot pie, pizza—"

"Enough!" cried the Poes.

Milly hesitated. She couldn't help herself. "Loganberry?"

The boys threw their hands in the air.

"My brain feels like it's all scrambled up!" Em said.

Edgar and Allan looked at her. "Your brain feels like it's what?" they asked.

"Scrambled up."

Then the boys turned to each other, smiling. "Of course! How could we have missed it?"

"Missed what?" Milly asked. "Is there a kind of pie I've left out?"

"It has nothing to do with pie," Allan said.

"Then what is it?"

"The three sentences consist of letters that are scrambled," Edgar explained.

"Like Em's brain?" Milly asked dryly.

"Anagrams," Allan elaborated. "And hidden in each is the same thing. The answer to our problem."

The girls looked again at the sentences.

Edgar and Allan had it now (using two minds as one is highly efficient):

I'll make a wise phrase. Unscrambled = William Shakespeare.

Hear me as I will speak. Unscrambled = William Shakespeare.

We shall make a pie, sir! Unscrambled = William Shakespeare.

Em and Milly applauded when the boys shared their discovery.

"Of course, we'd have figured it out too," Milly assured them.

"Given a little more time," added Em.

"Tomorrow night," Edgar announced, with growing excitement, "we'll go back to the cemetery and find a tomb that bears the name Shakespeare. And I'll wager that inside that tomb we'll discover not only the Lafitte brothers' treasure, but also Pierre's diary and the evidence we need to prove to the jury of history that he murdered our friends Clarence and Genevieve Du Valier in 1814."

"And then we'll make it public and, by doing so, we'll set the Du Valiers free to move on to the next world," Allan concluded.

WHAT THE POE TWINS DID NOT KNOW . . .

INTERNAL E-MAIL MESSAGE STRING:

From: Wender, Werner

To: Carmichel, Richard

Sent: Wed, 20 Nov, 11:51 p.m.

Subject: RE: PROBLEM

Mr. Carmichel,

Do you think I care if the personnel department has discovered a problem with the social security number of one of my crew members? Don't you realize that I finish shooting my film IN ONE DAY!!!! At this point, I do not care if she is using an "assumed name," so long as she gets her work done.

I am an artist! Do not waste my energy with administrative garbage.

W.W.

> **From:** Carmichel, Richard
>
> **To:** Wender, Werner

> **Sent:** Wed, 20 Nov, 4:54 p.m.

> **Subject:** PROBLEM

> Dear Mr. Wender,

> The Human Resources Department has dis-
> covered a problem in the file of your recently
> hired production assistant, Cassie Kilmer.
> Her name does not match her social security
> number. However, the number does match a
> Cassandra Perry, who is wanted by police in
> three states for fraud. We recommend that
> you immediately terminate her employment
> and contact the authorities.

> Sincerely,

> Richard Carmichel
> Director of Human Resources

Mr. Poe in the Great Beyond

Mr. Shakespeare approached Mr. Poe's cubicle with papers in his hand.

"Start packing up your desk, Poe."

"What?"

"Yes, it's off to the Animal Languages Division for you."

"*What?*"

With the tip of his quill pen, Mr. Shakespeare indicated the place on the paperwork where Homer had signed and approved the transfer.

"Animal languages?" Mr. Poe cried. "I write in English, sir. I might be willing to indulge my excellent Latin or adequate French if you ask nicely. But I will *not* write in zebra!"

The Animal Languages Division was about as low

as it could get for a writer here. *Oink, oink. Cluck, cluck.* It was one thing to communicate through fortune cookie fortunes or spell cryptic messages on car license plates or slip anachronistic speeches into movie scripts, as Mr. Poe had already done. But for a writer to have to communicate *without words?* He'd have been better off transferred to the Interpretive Dance Division (and, frankly, Mr. Poe was a terrible dancer).

Mr. Poe had begun to make a counterargument when Mr. Shakespeare stopped him with a raised index finger. "Please, Mr. Poe, try to maintain a shred of dignity and resist the temptation to beg for your position."

Mr. Poe gathered himself. He hadn't been about to beg (plead, perhaps). He set his shoulders, raised his chin, and resolved to demonstrate his own indomitable spirit. He started with a quote he recalled from somewhere. "'You speak a language that I understand not,'" he said, almost cheerfully. "'My life stands in the level of your dreams.'"

Mr. Shakespeare smirked. "I see you've no response of your own, Mr. Poe. Nonetheless, I commend you for choosing to quote from the best—me!"

Mr. Poe took a sharp breath.

"Now, pack up your desk and get down to the

Animal Languages Division. Oh, and by the way . . ." Mr. Shakespeare paused.

Mr. Poe waited.

"Hee-haw," said Mr. Shakespeare, grinning as he turned to go.

Smart-ass, Mr. Poe thought.

Later, Mr. Poe carried his cardboard box of pencils, pens, paper, and other office knickknacks (including his framed photographs of Edgar and Allan) toward the elevator. But on the way, he detoured to the isolated corner cubicle of the poet Emily Dickinson, a shy New Englander whose carefully crafted poems seethed with life and death. Mr. Poe had met her only once or twice, as she liked to keep to herself. But her dark eyes were quite beautiful.

She was employed now in the greeting card division.

"Miss Dickinson?" he inquired softly.

She looked up from her desk.

"May I have a moment of your time?"

With the slightest movement of her head, she indicated yes.

"I've been transferred," Mr. Poe explained.

"Upstairs or down?" she asked.

"Down."

She put her hand to her mouth. "How many floors?"

"Only about four hundred," he said reassuringly.

In a building 362 million floors tall, this wasn't the worst demotion possible (aggravating as it was to Mr. Poe).

"Oh, then perhaps we will meet again," she said, offering a shy smile.

"I hope so," he said. "In any case, before leaving I wanted to tell you how much I admire your strange but beautiful and brave poems."

Of course, Mr. Poe didn't think she was as great a poet as he was. But what was the point of saying something like that aloud?

"Strange. . . . Beautiful. . . . Brave. . . . Those words could describe your work as well, Mr. Poe."

He hadn't felt this good in almost two centuries. "Thank you."

Her expression turned serious. "Your lovely boys are in danger," she observed.

He nodded.

"And my lovely nieces have taken a liking to them," she continued.

"And vice versa, Miss Dickinson."

She sighed. "Isn't it a shame that rules prevent us from interfering in their perilous lives?"

But before he could answer, a voice rang out among the office cubicles.

"Poe, what are you still doing on this floor!" Mr. Shakespeare approached from across the hall. "This floor is for writers who use *language*. You belong downstairs among the grunts and squeals."

Miss Dickinson glared in the Bard's direction. "He *is* smug, wouldn't you say, my dear Mr. Poe?"

Mr. Poe smiled, despite his multitudinous worries.

"Poe!" Mr. Shakespeare shouted.

Anxious to preserve his last shred of dignity, especially in front of Miss Dickinson, Mr. Poe made a sweeping, courtly bow to her and slipped away from the cubicles and into the hallway, heading for the elevator, his box of desk supplies held loosely in his pale hands.

His face flushed pink.

A DREAM WITHIN A DREAM

THE Poe and Dickinson twins watched the brightening sky as the sun edged over the horizon.

What a night it had been. Ghosts, pirate treasure, plans . . .

They stood up from their places on the rooftop and stretched (Roderick, too).

"Look up," Em said, pointing. "There's one star that's brighter than all the others. Venus, perhaps?"

"Actually—" Allan began.

"I'll tell you what it is," Milly interrupted, taking out her phone. "I have this NASA app that'll identify it."

"But—" Edgar started.

"Just give me a second." She tapped and scrolled before pointing the phone up to the sky. "It'll beep when it's identified the object."

Seconds passed . . . and no beep.

Confused, Milly lowered the phone and looked at the screen. Then she glanced back up into the sky, baffled. "It says there's nothing up there. No planet. No star . . ."

"That's because it's an orbiting satellite," Edgar said.

"If you watch, you'll notice it moving very slowly across the sky," added Allan.

"I didn't know you could see satellites with the naked eye," Em said.

"You can if you know how to look."

The boys had been looking for the past seven years, ever since their parents' accidental launch into space. They regularly tracked the Bradbury Telecommunications Satellite, the orbiting tomb of their mother and father. They'd last seen it from a Kansas cornfield.

"Is that, um, your parents' satellite up there?" Milly asked delicately.

The girls knew the sad story of Mal and Irma Poe and the Atlas V rocket.

All of America knew it.

"No," Edgar said. "That's just an ordinary one."

"Oh, drat!" Allan groaned, glancing at his wristwatch. "We're due in the makeup trailer in forty-five minutes."

They'd been awake now for twenty-four hours straight.

Em grinned. "I suppose that's what you two get for being the 'stars' of the last scene."

"Our scenes are done," Milly added, smiling mischievously. "But we'll be thinking of you this morning while *we* catch up on sleep.

In response, the boys could only yawn.

By eleven a.m., the Poe twins still had not started shooting their scene. They'd suffered through the familiar makeup routine, climbed into their stiff-collared costumes, shuffled to the buffet table to smear cream cheese on bagels for breakfast, and arrived on the set on time. But since then . . . nothing, as the lighting crew struggled to get a particular effect that Mr. Wender insisted upon.

"I want it perfect!" he shouted.

Some among the crew whispered that the director's reluctance to shoot had less to do with lighting than it did with his dissatisfaction with the script. Set in a luxurious, nineteenth-century parlor, the scene was written as a fantasy sequence in which the boys sipped tea and argued about good and evil—two sides of their famous ancestor. But it lacked punch.

It was the final scene in the movie, the all-important closing. And Mr. Wender still hadn't come up with any improvements.

So the lighting crew was getting an education in German cuss words.

Meantime, the Poe twins caught up on shut-eye, one on the set's velvet, nineteenth-century divan, the other in the big wingback chair beside the fireplace.

At last, Cassie shouted, "Everyone to their places!"

But Edgar and Allan remained in a deep snooze.

"What is this sleeping?" Mr. Wender shouted, drawing everyone's attention.

That is, everyone except the twin objects of his anger, who merely began to snore more loudly.

"What in Gott's name are you two doing?" Mr. Wender raged, slamming his copy of the script to the ground.

At last, the twins opened their eyes.

The director strode toward them. "I do not tolerate sleeping on the set!"

Edgar sat up on the divan. "We weren't just sleeping," he said.

"No?" Mr. Wender pressed.

The twins thought fast.

"Um, we were sharing a dream," Allan said as he straightened in the wingback chair and ran his hand through his cowlicks (identical to his brother's cowlicks, naturally).

"Sharing one dream?" Mr. Wender scoffed. "How is it I didn't guess that straight off?"

"Oh, don't be too hard on yourself," Allan said, ignoring the director's sarcasm. He stood, fluffing the high collar of his nineteenth-century shirt and tugging at the ridiculous satin pants. "Do you want to hear about our dream?"

"No!" Mr. Wender snapped, stalking away.

"You might find it inspirational for the final scene," Edgar added.

After a few steps the director stopped and turned back. "Well . . . maybe."

Allan nodded graciously. "In the dream, we were the young Edgar Allan Poe, our great-great-great-great grand-uncle, just like in the movie."

"That's of no help."

"But instead of sipping tea, we were sitting in this very room doing . . ."

"Doing what?" Mr. Wender inquired.

Mr. Wender needed a better ending and the Poe twins needed a little more sleep.

Crew members began to gather around the boys.

"In the dream, what were you doing?" Mr. Wender pressed.

Since the twins hadn't been dreaming at all, this was no easy question.

Stumped, Edgar and Allan looked at each other.

Hadn't Em said something about a trick she employed whenever she was stumped by a question, something that both enlivened and cleared her mind?

But what *was* it?

"Chess pie!" Edgar exclaimed.

The director looked at them as if they had spoken in a foreign language. "What?"

"We mean—um, chess!" Allan said.

"Yes, we were"—Edgar slowly rose from the divan, playing for time—"we were playing chess on a beautiful luminescent board."

Mr. Wender snapped to attention. "Go on."

"Naturally, the chess game was very symbolic," Edgar continued. "The black versus the white, representing the two sides of our famous great-great-great-great granduncle."

Mr. Wender pursed his lips and then shook his head. "That's been done before. It's overworked."

"But there was more to the dream!" Allan insisted.

They knew Poe's life as well as they knew their own.

The director sighed as if disinterested, but indicated with a wave of his hand for the twins to continue.

"See, as we moved the pieces on the board, we didn't talk about good and evil, as in the script, but about how much we missed our mother and father," Edgar said.

"Hmmm," Mr. Wender mused, growing more interested. "Yes, Poe *was* orphaned at a young age."

Like us, the boys thought.

"And then, at the very end of the dream," Allan continued, infusing his voice with drama, "we realized that both the black and the white chess sets were missing their kings and queens and had been missing them *all along*."

Mr. Wender's eyes widened.

"Naturally, this prompted us to wonder: 'Exactly what kind of chess game have we been playing?'" finished Edgar.

The twins waited for the director to answer the question.

"A mysterious chess game," Mr. Wender muttered. He looked up, inspired. "A game that could be neither won nor lost!"

"Because it lacked the king and queen," Allan said.

Mr. Wender whispered in German, *"Die Mutter und der Vater . . ."*

"Exactly," Edgar and Allan answered in unison.

The boys' famous ancestor hadn't been lucky enough to be adopted by loving relatives who accepted him for who he was.

Edgar and Allan thought of Uncle Jack and Aunt Judith.

The Poe twins knew they'd been luckier than their great-great-great-great granduncle.

"By the end of our dream," Allan said, "we understood a lot more about Edgar Allan Poe's life."

"All the ups and downs that are in your movie, Mr. Wender," Edgar added.

Mr. Wender nodded. He closed his eyes and took a deep breath. "I could cut to a close-up of the chess board," he said to himself. Then he opened his eyes. "Yes, the final shot of the movie!" A wide grin spread across his face. He slapped the Poe brothers on their shoulders and then turned to the crew, raising his voice. "Call the prop master! I need a luminescent chess board. And we'll be changing the whole lighting setup."

The crew snapped to action.

Mr. Wender turned back to Edgar and Allan. "That was quite a useful dream, boys." He squinted suspiciously. "Wait a minute. Did you say you *shared* a dream?"

This was no time to get into all that.

Besides, there'd been no dream.

"No big deal," the boys said in unison.

"Aren't they little geniuses?" Cassie commented, hovering about the set.

Mr. Wender nodded and turned away, starting toward the lighting crew, calling out his new directions.

Edgar returned to the divan.

Allan returned to the chair.

Zzzzzz . . .

That afternoon—after Mr. Wender shouted, "Cut and print! That's a wrap!" and the crew cheered and clapped Edgar and Allan on their backs—the Poe twins stopped in the lobby of the Pepper Tree Inn to send a postcard to their school friends.

To all,

Don't be fooled. Moviemaking is not all fun and games. But that's not to say we aren't having a great time here in New Orleans. Last night in the city's oldest cemetery, we made new friends, Clarence and Genevieve. Actually, they live in the cemetery. Well, maybe "live" isn't the right word. Anyway, we'll explain when we get back to school. And speaking of school . . . now that Mr. Mann has been fired, how's the new principal?

Most sincerely,
E and A and Roderick

P.S. We also made friends with another set of twins, Em and Milly. We think you'd like them. We do.

The Seventh Grade
Edwin "Buzz" Aldrin Middle School
345 Carmello Court
Baltimore, MD 21215

WHAT THE POE TWINS DID NOT KNOW . . .

A RECEIPT IN CASSIE'S HANDBAG:

JACKSON DRUG STORE
3211 W. Diego St.
New Orleans, LA 70116
225-555-4938

----

1 bottle Rat Poison	$6.49
1 pack Syringes	$7.74

Tax	$1.28
Total	$15.51

HAVE A NICE DAY!

BACK TO THE BONEYARD

THE boys were well rested when they returned to the Saint Louis Cemetery late that night. Once again, Uncle Jack and Aunt Judith had lingered over evening tea in the lobby of the Pepper Tree Inn, so Edgar, Allan, and Roderick had climbed out of their room window, crawled across the ledge, and shinned down the balcony to the alley.

This time, however, they were not met by the Dickinson sisters.

Instead, Em and Milly were engaged now in their own part of the mission, which was to find a way to break into the New Orleans Pirate Museum, where the wax figures of the Lafitte brothers highlighted the collection of buccaneer memorabilia.

And that wasn't the only difference between this late-night trip to the cemetery and the first.

Tonight, Allan and Edgar did not run but strolled casually, hoping to make the pickax, shovel, and pair of

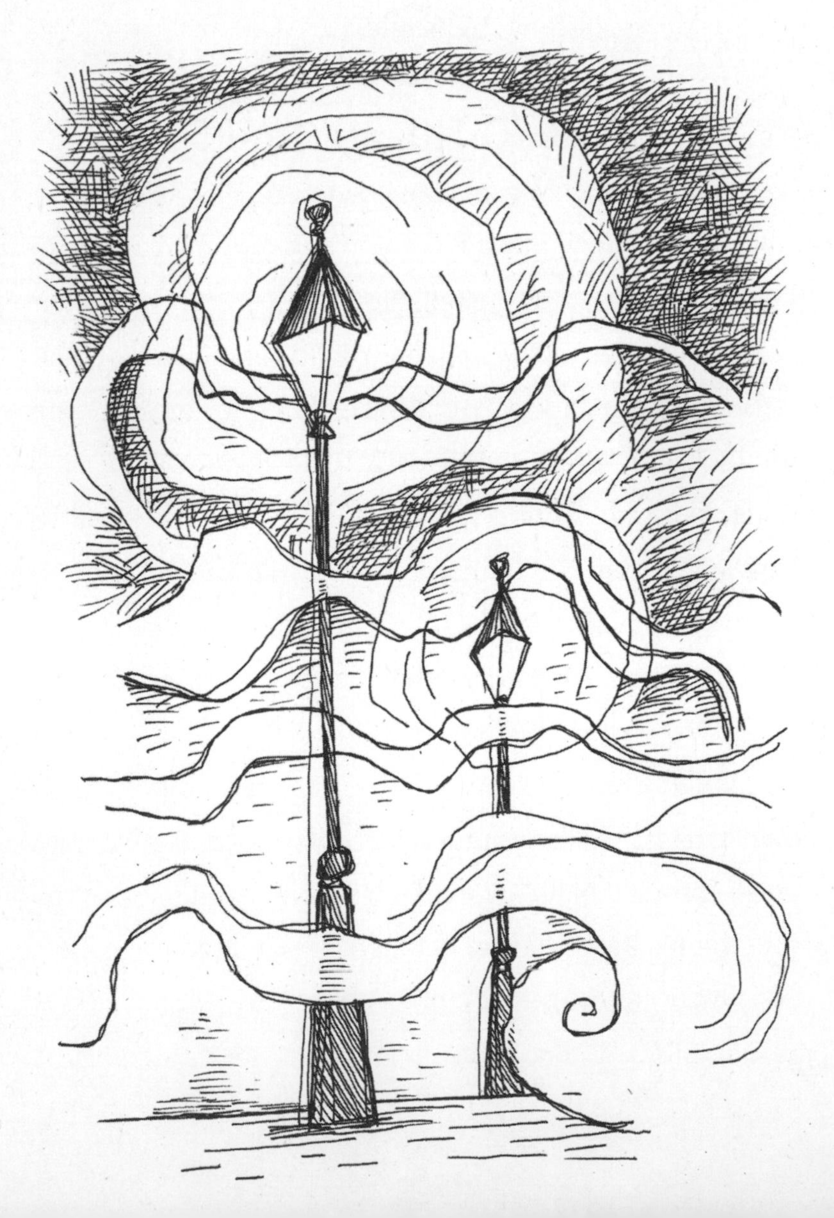

flashlights they'd bought that afternoon at a hardware store seem less suspicious to passersby.

And the weather was different. Thick fog had rolled up the river and now blanketed the French Quarter, limiting visibility to about twenty feet. The bright lights of the crowded streets looked like colorful galaxies viewed through an out-of-focus telescope. And as the twins left the tourist district and neared the cemetery, the dimmer, less frequently spaced streetlamps cast strange halos over the otherwise encompassing dark.

Finally, this trip to the cemetery was different because Allan and Edgar had a worrisome sense of being followed, though each time they turned back no one was there. Even Roderick looked over his shoulder from time to time.

The cemetery awaited in stillness.

The boys and cat edged through the break in the wall.

A cemetery that is spooky on a clear night is spookier on a foggy one. But Edgar and Allan were not particularly spooked.

Their first stop was the tomb of their friends.

The memorial stone was different from how it had been just the day before.

MADAME GENEVIEVE DU VALIER
HERE LIES OUR SISTER
BELOVED WIFE
MAY SHE REST IN PEACE WITH OUR
LORD FOREVER
DIED OCTOBER 1, 1814
MONSIEUR CLARENCE DU VALIER
HERE LIES OUR BROTHER
BELOVED HUSBAND
MAY HE REST IN MERCIFUL AND
HONORABLY RIGHTEOUS SLUMBER
DIED OCTOBER 1, 1814

No worn-away letters . . . a night off for Genevieve and Clarence.

But the Poe twins' work had just begun.

Edgar and Allan split up to scour the cemetery, looking for a mausoleum marked SHAKESPEARE. Just twenty-four hours earlier, they might have been startled by the occasional wisps of fog that crept in ghostly shapes around the corners and cornices of the stone crypts. But since meeting the Du Valiers, Edgar and Allan had learned that real ghosts looked more like ordinary human beings than ectoplasm.

Continuing up and down the long rows, the twins took note of all the tombs they passed, resting places for families with names like Petit, Moreau, Martinez, Laurent, Bertrand, Fournier, Morel, Girard, Mercier, Garcia, Bonnet, Lopez, Blanc, Mathieu, Gautier, Dumont, Fontaine, Sanchez, Marchand, Dufour, Dumas, Leroux, Renard, Dupuis, Laveau, de Tremblement, Gomez, Leblanc . . .

Then Edgar and Allan met one another coming around a fog-enshrouded corner.

"I think we've covered the whole cemetery," Edgar said.

"Lots of French surnames with a little Spanish tossed in," added Allan.

"That pretty well describes the population of New Orleans in the early 1800s."

But they hadn't come here to take a census.

The bottom line was that there was no Shakespeare crypt.

Not even any names of his major characters. No Hamlet or Lear or Macbeth or Capulet or Montague or Othello . . .

Had Edgar and Allan figured it wrong?

The boys looked at each other, their two minds working as one.

After a moment, each broke out laughing.

Five minutes later, Edgar and Allan arrived with their pickax and shovel at the weathered but otherwise ordinary-looking tomb of a man named Lance de Tremblement, who died in 1813. As they struck at the old brass doors, they couldn't help but wonder how they'd walked past it the first time.

It was so simple!

After all, the Lafitte brothers' native language was French.

And in French the word lance means "spear," while *tremblement* means "tremor" or "shaking." Thus "Lance de Tremblement," in English, was "a spear of shaking" or a "Shake-spear"!

Crack!

The boys broke the lock on the metal doors.

Allan tossed the pickax aside.

They looked at one another. Neither had ever entered a tomb at midnight before.

What awaited them in the darkness?

With Roderick serving as lookout, the twins entered the ominous crypt. They flicked on their flashlights, running the beams over the small cobwebbed chamber.

No skeletons, no coffins, no cremation urns.

There was nothing there at all.

The boys looked at each other in dismay. Had they guessed wrong?

"Any self-respecting pirate would make this a little more difficult," Allan murmured.

They did a second flashlit examination of the crypt . . . and still, nothing.

Then, from a darkened corner, Roderick meowed.

"What is it?" Edgar asked.

Roderick meowed again, this time more urgently, his eyes reflecting the flashlights' beams.

The boys rushed over.

Roderick sat atop a stone slab, which looked like a blank grave marker. After a moment, he inclined his head graciously, rose to his feet, stretched, and padded off.

The boys examined the slab. Then they reached for their pickax and shovel.

Any pirate worth his reputation *always* buried his treasure.

Edgar levered up the slab with the pickax. Allan began to dig.

And after several frantic minutes, they broke through to a subterranean storage space.

Within it was pirate treasure—far more than two boys could carry.

They opened the first of a half dozen chests, all of which had been waterproofed with tar.

Inside, glittering gold doubloons, booty of the Spanish Main!

In the second chest were more doubloons; in the third and fourth were jewels, sparkling in colors that hadn't faded in two centuries; in the fifth were heavy serving dishes and chalices, all layered in gold and studded with rubies; in the sixth were personal items, such as clothing, boots of Spanish leather, hats, swords, and, most important:

A leather-bound diary stored inside of a sealskin pouch.

Edgar opened it, with Allan's flashlight trained upon the first page.

A few minutes later, when the Poe twins emerged from the tomb, they still bore the wide grins that had spread across their faces when they first spied the treasure. But grins aside, they looked quite different from before. Now, they wore feathered pirate hats, vests that smelled of gunpowder even two centuries after their last use, and, slung across their hips, scabbards with slightly rusted swords—all authentic pirate loot. Roderick sported a two-hundred-year-old silk scarf around his neck.

Aside from the pirate garb and accessories, the twins had taken from the crypt only the murderous pirate's incriminating diary. They closed the brass doors behind them, picked up their tools, and covered their tracks so no one would stumble across their discovery before the proper authorities were notified.

The boys might be dressed like pirates. But they weren't really interested in loot.

This was about justice.

They ran out of the cemetery and back into the crowded part of the French Quarter. Here, every night was like a masquerade party, so their unusual attire (including swords) drew hardly any attention.

At the museum, they found the Dickinson sisters crouched in shadows near the entrance.

"Did you get the diary?" Em whispered.

Edgar and Allan's faces answered the question.

"And in it he confesses his crime?" Milly asked.

"In gory detail," said Allan.

"Good. But we're not going to be able to break in tonight. So Milly and I have come up with a plan B."

"Why can't we go tonight?" the Poe twins asked impatiently.

Milly pointed to the museum. Inside, the lights were on. "There's a whole crew in there, getting ready for a show that opens tomorrow."

"Look at the banner they just hung to advertise it," Em added.

"I have a feeling that show's not going to run for long," Edgar said.

The next morning, plan B worked like this:

With Uncle Jack and Aunt Judith breakfasting with Em and Milly's parents back at the hotel, the Poe and Dickinson twins stood near the front of the line as the New Orleans Pirate Museum opened its doors. Once inside, they browsed the centuries-old skull-and-crossbones flags, the rusty swords, and the weathered treasure chests, trying to look like ordinary tourists.

But, of course, the Poe and Dickinson twins were in no way "ordinary."

"Ready?" Milly asked the boys.

Edgar and Allan looked around the museum. The crowd had thickened, this being the opening day of the show.

Allan nodded. "It's time."

The quartet moved from the first room to the larger, windowless room where the wax figures of the Lafitte brothers stood.

"Time for you to get yours," Edgar muttered to Pierre's wax figure.

Nearby stood a glass case containing personal items

that had once belonged to the murderous Pierre: comb, razor, compass, hat, sword.

"You think that's the sword he used to run through our friends?" Em asked.

"Could be," answered Allan.

Edgar turned to Milly. "Ready?"

She nodded briskly and produced her phone. Then she tapped on the keyboard, entering a string of Internet commands to reach the control panel of the museum's power and security system. Next, she bypassed the password, which she'd cracked the night before while the boys were occupied in the cemetery.

"The password is, 'Ahoy Matey,'" she whispered, disgruntled that it had been so easy. "An amateur could have broken in. I feel kind of insulted."

"How long will we have?" Allan asked.

"We'll have fifteen seconds between the time the power goes down and the backup generator kicks in, so we'll have to act fast," Em said. "Everybody ready?"

Milly showed the phone to Edgar and Allan. "How does this algorithm look to you?"

"Great," the boys said.

She grinned and pushed the button.

Later that afternoon, the Poe and Dickinson twins sat in the otherwise unoccupied lobby of the Pepper Tree Inn, watching local news on an old console TV.

"What's so important on the tube?" Uncle Jack inquired as he came downstairs from a nap.

"Current events," they muttered.

"Hi, kids," Aunt Judith said, walking into the lobby with the Dickinson twins' parents, Blossom and Claude, who were philosophy professors at Johns Hopkins University in Baltimore.

"So, is everyone well?" inquired Mrs. Dickinson, who the boys had noticed upon first meeting had a cool Phoenician symbol tattooed on her neck.

The two sets of twins answered with nods, their attention still on the TV.

Mr. Dickinson, who was bearded and wore a black turtleneck sweater, said, "Now, you girls know we allow *no television.*"

The Poe family had no such rules.

Just then the TV news show cut to a big graphic that read:

Instead of turning off the TV, the Poe twins turned it up.

A serious-looking newsman announced:

"This is Ryan Holborn with new details about this morning's shocking invasion of the New Orleans Pirate Museum. According to New Orleans police, intruders vandalized a wax figure and broke into a glass case during a momentary power outage."

The TV cut to a shot of the figure of Pierre Lafitte, dressed not in his pirate garb but instead in the striped outfit of a jailed convict (bought the night before by the Dickinson twins at a costume shop near the Pepper Tree Inn).

"But the wax figure is not what makes this story

so shocking," continued the news anchor. "It's that the unknown suspects took nothing from the museum, but instead *left behind* a valuable, pirate-related artifact, which has been authenticated over the past few hours. Live with us now is the New Orleans Pirate Museum's curator, Ellen Payne. Thank you for joining us, Miss Payne."

The news feed cut to a live shot of a blonde woman in a red scarf standing outside the museum.

"Miss Payne, can you tell us anything about the historical item left behind in the broken glass case?" asked the newsman.

For someone whose museum had just been invaded, she seemed remarkably happy. "It is the handwritten diary of Pierre Lafitte!"

The two sets of twins leaned toward the TV.

"And that diary is financially valuable?" the reporter queried.

"Oh, yes," Miss Payne answered brightly. "And, better yet, the diary sheds new historical light on some of the most important figures of the period. For example, we found it open to a page upon which Lafitte confessed in his own hand to the cold-blooded killing of a local couple named . . ." She glanced down at the old leather diary in her hand.

"Say it, say it. . . ." muttered the Poe twins, anxiously.

"Let's see," Miss Payne continued, her eyes scanning the small, ornate handwriting.

"Come on!" the Dickinson twins shouted at the TV. "Say their names!"

"What's going on here, kids?" Aunt Judith asked.

"His victims' name was Du Valier," the museum curator said at last. "Clarence and Genevieve, whom he murdered in cold blood outside their own pub in 1814."

At these words, Edgar, Allan, Em, and Milly looked at each other, then stood and cheered, thrusting their fists in the air, victorious.

Their guardians watched them as if they were insane.

"What's this all about?" Uncle Jack asked.

Aunt Judith and Mr. and Mrs. Dickinson looked just as confused.

"Justice!" the four twins answered as one.

WHAT THE POE TWINS DID NOT KNOW . . .

CELL PHONE TEXT MESSAGES BETWEEN
NATASHA PERRY AND CASSANDRA PERRY:

Arriving at New Orleans Union Passenger Terminal on the 6:10. Aren't these modern phones amazing?

I'll be there to pick you up, Grandmother.

THAT'S A WRAP!

THAT evening, before leaving the hotel room for *A Tale of Poe*'s wrap party, Allan and Edgar tuned the TV to the Wild Animal Channel, which was broadcasting its annual Bird Week Marathon. While the boys preferred Predator Week, nothing appealed more to Roderick than watching parakeets flutter from branch to branch. He watched it the way gourmets watch the Food Channel. Additionally, Bird Week allowed the cat to perfect his many vocal impressions, which he sometimes used to lure tasty between-meal snacks in the tree branches outside the Poes' house.

"Your dish is filled with sparkling water," Allan told Roderick, who preferred it to still.

"And your food bowl is over here," Edgar said, indicating the Cajun tuna tartare they'd ordered up from the room service menu.

Roderick nodded, though his eyes remained on the TV.

The Poe twins had felt bad when Cassie informed them that pets were not allowed in the fancy restaurant Mr. Wender had rented for the festivities.

At first, the boys considered skipping the party.

But Roderick had curled up on the bed and looked like he could use a quiet night anyway.

"We ordered special sheets," Edgar told him.

"Egyptian cotton with a thread count of a thousand!" Allan added.

Roderick turned to them and then chirped like a parakeet.

"So you'll be OK while we're out?" the Poe twins inquired.

Roderick answered by cawing like a crow.

"Good," the boys said.

They closed the window and double-checked the lock on the door after them.

The wrap party was going strong by the time the Poe family arrived at the restaurant. The Dixieland jazz playing inside, rollicking and free and fun, lured tourists from all over the French Quarter. But five burly security guards saw to it that only invited guests got in.

"Yes, here you are," a security guard said to the Poe family as he checked a list at the door. "VIPs."

The prop crew had redecorated the restaurant with some of the Poe-oriented props used in the movie. A stuffed raven perched at the end of the bar. Mannequins in medieval masquerade garb stood scattered around the room. A giant silhouette of a black cat served as the backdrop to the band playing on a makeshift stage.

In the soft red light it all might have come off as spooky.

But the music kept it upbeat.

"Ah, my Poe family!" Mr. Wender said, approaching them with his arms open wide. "Welcome!"

Uncle Jack shook his hand.

"Help yourselves to our buffet," the director directed.

"You're the boss!" Uncle Jack answered gleefully.

The Dickinson family approached the Poes from across the room.

Em wore her usual long frock with a high, lacy collar. She always looked nice, if a little out-of-date. The surprise was that Milly also wore a dress (more modern). This was the first time the boys had seen her in anything besides either her movie costume or jeans and a T-shirt.

"It's kind of a special occasion," Milly explained.

"You mean finishing the movie?" Edgar asked her. "The wrap party?"

"No," she said, looking away. "I mean it's our last night all together."

"Oh, yeah," Allan said, suddenly shy.

Then the music stopped and Mr. Wender joined the band on the stage, holding up one hand to quiet the room.

The din of conversation ceased.

In his other hand, the director held a glass of champagne. "I want to toast everyone here tonight," he said. "You're a top-notch crew and cast. And I particularly want to thank my baby Poes, Edgar and Allan, for helping me to devise a perfect ending for our film." He raised his glass higher. *"Prost!"*

German for "cheers."

"Prost!" called those in the room with drinks.

Edgar and Allan smiled graciously.

"And I want to thank my dedicated new assistant, Cassie Kilmer, who was such a help to me the last few days here in New Orleans. Cassie?"

Everyone looked around the room.

"Should I say 'Cassandra Perry'?" Mr. Wender continued lightly. "Oh, what a complication you've been to our accountants, my dear. But, by any name, I want to toast you as a girl who understands the value of punctuality. Where are you, Cassie?"

She wasn't there.

The Poe twins looked at each other, possessed by a sudden, terrible thought.

Cassandra *Perry*?

Like Professor *Perry*?

Meantime, Mr. Wender gestured for the band to start playing again.

The Dixieland jazz kicked in.

Then the Poe twins spotted the makeup lady cradling her Chihuahua and, across the room, the script supervisor holding her Cavalier King Charles spaniel, and they realized that pets *weren't* forbidden here after all. It had been a lie.

Roderick was alone!

Edgar and Allan darted out of the restaurant, into the crowded streets of the French Quarter, and back toward their hotel.

The Poe twins threw open the door.

Their hotel room looked like it had been tossed into a giant dryer and run through the spin cycle.

"Roderick?" they called in unison.

The two mattresses and all the bedding had been stripped and scattered, shredded by what appeared to have been sharp and furious cat claws. The flowered wallpaper was newly decorated with vertical stripes that bore the signature of a violently frantic feline putting up a good fight. The latest volumes in the boys' favorite book series, True Stories of Horror, lay scattered about the room, looking as if they'd been run through a paper shredder.

But no Roderick.

The boys glanced into the bathroom. It, too, was a mess, but absent any living thing.

Then they noticed the TV. They'd left it tuned to the Bird Week Marathon, but that's not what occupied the screen now.

Instead, they saw Cassie's face. "Hello, boys," she said, sweet as pralines.

They'd been played for fools!

"By now, you've realized I have your little friend Roderick."

The twins drew nearer to the TV, despite the sinking feeling they felt in their guts.

"You may have questions," Cassandra Perry continued. "For example, what could I possibly have against you two? But we can leave all that for when we're together in person." She paused, then flashed her cover girl smile, which this time seemed to take up half the TV screen. "Oh, yes, we will meet soon. And in the meantime, you'll do exactly as I say. That is, if you ever want to see your cat again, alive."

Edgar and Allan resolved never to let Roderick out of their sight from that moment on.

"You will return to the cemetery," she continued, her blue eyes boring into them. "Not tomorrow morning—not in an hour—but *now*. And don't pretend you don't know which cemetery. The one I followed you to. Oh, I wasn't about to let you sneak out of the hotel unattended two nights in a row. But in the fog I lost track of you, though I heard mention of a treasure in a tomb. Which one?"

The boys thought, as one, *We have a bargaining chip. We can trade the crypt's location for Roderick.*

"And don't contact the police—or your aunt and uncle, unless you want to put them six feet underground," she continued. "Nor anyone else, like that other set of twins I've had to put up with the last couple days." She stopped. After a moment, she softened her voice, which served only to make it more sinister. "I'll see you soon, boys. Unless, of course, you choose to let your cat friend die."

The video froze, then hissed, smoked, and self-destructed, as in spy movies.

It seemed there was more to Cassie than the boys had imagined.

For the third time in three nights, Edgar and Allan climbed through the crack in the wall of the silent Saint Louis Cemetery. By the light of a full moon, the place looked the same, though it had never felt lonelier. Now there was no Roderick for companionship (though the boys trusted he was nearby), and no Dickinson sisters for conversation. Even the Du Valiers had likely moved on. And when the last of the dead leave a cemetery, it becomes a lonely place indeed.

And, tonight, a dangerous one too.

The Poe twins carried the rusted antique swords they had taken from the tomb of Lance de Tremblement the night before. Two centuries had dulled the blades, but any weapons were better than none.

"Cassie?" Allan called into the darkness. "We're here. Where are you?"

No answer.

"Cassie?" Edgar shouted. "Give us Roderick and we'll tell you where to find the treasure."

Silence. Then a shuffling sound.

The twins whirled around—but it was just a rat scurrying away between tombs.

"Cassie?"

"The name's Cassandra, boys," came a woman's voice from a few rows away.

The twins started in the direction of the voice. They said nothing, creeping silently, hoping to take her by surprise.

However, they were the ones surprised.

"Freeze, boys." The voice was behind them. "Now turn, slowly."

It was Cassie. But hadn't they just heard her in the distance?

The boys drew their swords as they turned.

Cassie held Roderick in one arm, squeezed tight. In her free hand she held a syringe, pointed at Roderick's furry neck. "Lose the swords, silly boys, or he gets it."

"What's in the syringe?" Edgar asked.

"Death," she answered.

The boys believed her. They had no choice but to drop their swords, which fell to the ground with a rusty clatter.

"Look, we know you're related to the professor," Allan said. "Are you working for him?"

"I'm his daughter, and I'm working *against* him!" she snapped.

"Then that puts us on the same side," Edgar observed reasonably.

She shook her head. "Not exactly."

The boys shared a moment of bafflement.

"Tell me the name of the tomb that contains the treasure," Cassie continued.

"And then you'll give us Roderick?" Edgar asked.

"Well, the name of the tomb is actually just the first thing I'll be wanting from you two."

"And then what?"

"Let's take it one thing at a time," she said.

The boys shared another, less baffled thought.

"Otherwise you'll kill Roderick?" Allan asked.

She tightened her grip and their cat yowled. "Obviously."

"Wow, that's cold," Edgar said. "In fact, it's *downright frozen*."

And on cue, Roderick went stiff, his eyes fixed and glassy.

Cassie glanced down at the seemingly lifeless object she held against her body. A dead cat! Her eyes widened in panic.

"Hey, you scared him to death!" Allan said.

"He must have had a heart attack!" added Edgar.

Startled, she dropped both the "corpse" and the syringe.

"Threatening to kill a dead cat is no threat at all," Allan observed calmly as he picked up his sword.

She looked confused. "What, you're not even sad he's dead?"

Edgar snapped his fingers.

Roderick snapped back to life, leaping to the boys' side.

"What!" Cassie shouted, outraged.

The boys moved forward with swords extended.

"I think it's time we have a talk with the police," Edgar said.

"I don't think so, boys," announced another voice from behind them.

They turned.

An old woman stepped out of the shadows. She pointed a double-barreled shotgun at the Poe twins. It must have been *her* voice they'd heard calling to them.

"Drop your weapons."

Her face looked familiar. She was an older female version of Professor Perry.

The boys' swords clattered once more to the ground.

"Good timing, Grandmother," Cassie said, regaining her composure.

The old woman smiled at the twins. If anything, this was possibly the most terrifying sight of all. "Yes," she said. "I'm mother to your nemesis. And I hate him even more than you two."

Edgar and Allan looked at each other.

"Excuse my forwardness," Allan said to her, "but your last sentence was grammatically unclear. Do you mean you hate the professor even more than we hate him, or that you hate him even more than you hate us?"

"I don't hate you boys," she said.

"Oh, good," they responded.

"But I'm still going to have to ask you two to step into that open tomb," she said, nodding toward iron doors ajar on a mausoleum nearby.

The boys had been too distracted to notice it before.

"Why?" Allan asked.

"Because my granddaughter and I are going to seal you inside," she answered. "With mortar."

The twins thought of their great-great-great-great granduncle's famous story "The Cask of Amontillado," in which a villain traps his rival behind a brick wall. The story doesn't end well for the character behind the wall.

"Why would you do that to us?"

"Because my loathsome son considers you two to be irreplaceable to his 'great experiment,'" she answered. "You know his plan, boys. To kill one of you and imprison the other, and then to use your psychic connection as a channel between this world and the next. All for his own gain!"

She had it right.

"So, if you're opposed to that, why are you holding a gun on us?" Allan asked, reasonably.

"Because killing you *both*, right now, will make a waste of his life!" she answered, her eyes gleaming with devilish delight. "By demolishing his ambitions I'll demonstrate that his mother is quite capable of avenging a betrayal."

"And it'll also show that his long-abandoned daughter is someone to take seriously," Cassie added, having regained her poise.

What a family! the boys thought.

"Look, the professor is thousands of miles away," Edgar said. "He's hunted by authorities. He'll never show his face in the country again! So why bother with us?"

"Oh, he'll be back," Grandmother Perry answered.

"But we've already defeated him," Allan said.

"No, you've only delayed him," Cassie snapped. "But Grandmother and I *can* defeat him."

"Now get into the tomb," Grandmother Perry demanded, motioning with the shotgun. "And no more tricks with the cat."

The boys were stumped.

"No more stalling!" Grandmother Perry shouted.

And then, appearing from out of the shadows . . .

. . . were Clarence and Genevieve Du Valier.

"Are you harassing these boys?" Clarence asked Grandmother Perry.

"Where'd *you* come from?" the old woman demanded, turning and looking the mysterious couple up and down. "Masqueraders," she murmured. "Poor timing. . . . Looks like I'll have to put you do-gooders in the tomb along with the boys."

"I don't think so," Genevieve said sweetly. "We've just spent two centuries in a tomb and we're not anxious for more."

"In fact, it was these boys who set us free," Clarence said, smiling.

"What are you talking about?" Grandmother Perry snapped.

"It's a long story," Clarence said. "Why don't I just show you?" At this, he removed his head, cradling it in his arms.

Genevieve removed her head, too, for good measure.

And, unlike last time, blood gushed from the gaping wounds, cascading over their shoulders, drenching their bodies.

Even the Poe twins were taken aback.

Grandmother Perry gasped, clutched at her heart, and fell to the ground, unconscious.

Cassie screamed at the sight of the decapitated pair. She turned to run. But the headless Clarence blocked the path to the left, and the headless Genevieve blocked it to the right. Panicked, Cassie dodged into the open tomb.

The twins slammed the door behind her.

They wedged it shut but skipped the mortar. Instead, they'd let the police know where to find her.

The old couple put their heads back on their shoulders. (It made communicating so much easier.) The blood that had covered their clothes turned luminescent and then disappeared. They were their old selves once more.

"That was impressive," Edgar said to the Du Valiers.

"We thought you two had already moved on," Allan added.

"We wanted to thank you first," Clarence said.

"Besides, we were a little worried about that young woman, Cassie, who's been following you around the French Quarter," Genevieve added.

"Following us around?" the twins responded, aggrieved not to have noticed.

"Don't feel bad," Genevieve said. "She was stealthy.

And some things are just easier for ghosts to observe."

"In any case, we wanted to return the kind favor you did us," Clarence added.

"Well, you did," the boys chimed. "Thanks!"

"What will you two do now?" Genevieve asked.

Allan gestured toward the unconscious old woman, and then to the locked tomb that contained Cassie. "First we'll tie Grandma up, and then see that the police cart these two away."

"And then we'll deliver the treasure to the New Orleans Pirate Museum," Edgar added.

"And you two?" Allan asked.

Clarence and Genevieve smiled.

"Oh, we'll be moving on now, thank you," Clarence said.

When Genevieve kissed the boys on their cheeks, it felt to each like the merest breeze.

WHAT THE POE TWINS DID NOT KNOW . . .

AN UNMAILED LETTER RECOVERED BY POLICE IN THE HANDBAG OF MRS. NATASHA PERRY:

Dear Son,

I was grateful for your latest coded correspondence, as it has allowed me to contact you while you're in hiding. I'm quite sure that you're taking excellent measures to avoid detection. And I know you plan at some point to re-enter the USA. However, I am delighted to inform you that you needn't do so. See, there's no longer any reason. Your Poe twins are no more.

If you want to pay your respects, you may visit Saint Louis Cemetery in New Orleans, where you'll find them in a tomb marked with the name Gomez. Of course, by the time you arrive, all that will be left of them will be skeletons.

So much for your megalomaniacal plan! Remember, it was I who taught you to be devious. And I remain supreme. You and your quantum physics—ha!

Mother

P.S. And that all goes double for me, Father!

Yours, Cassandra

CELEBRATION

TWO days later, Edgar and Allan Poe settled behind the big semicircular desk on the set of the third-best-rated TV morning news program in New Orleans. The top two shows, *Rise and Shine, New Orleans!* and *Wake Up, New Orleans!*, had turned down exclusive interviews, still angry about the on-air confusion the twins had caused a few days before. No matter. Edgar and Allan knew that whatever show they appeared on now was bound to make national news.

"Welcome to *Sunrise New Orleans!*" said the host as the red light on the TV camera lit.

His hair wasn't as perfect as the host's hair at WKEU, and his posture wasn't as straight as the hostess's at WJRT. But his teeth glittered whiter than any Edgar and Allan had ever seen on a human being. The boys almost needed sunglasses to ward off the glamorous glare.

"It's my pleasure this morning to welcome Edgar and Allan Poe," he continued.

"Thanks," the boys said in unison.

"But don't forget Roderick Usher," Allan added.

The cat poked his head out from Edgar's jacket. He looked sleepy, which was no wonder, considering the schedule they'd all kept the past few days.

"Hello, Roderick," said the host graciously. Then he turned to the camera. "Just two days ago, these boys—the great-great-great-great grandnephews of the illustrious Edgar Allan Poe—finished shooting the upcoming Werner Wender film, *A Tale of Poe*. But that's not why they're here this morning." He turned back to the boys. "Tell our viewers how your actions resulted in the arrest of Cassandra Perry, a con artist wanted by police in three states, and her grandmother, a parolee whose gun violations will send her back to prison as soon as she's out of the hospital."

"Well, we used a two-pronged approach," Allan answered, like the veteran crime fighter he was quickly becoming.

"First we employed the Stuffed Cat," Edgar said.

"The what?" the host asked.

"It's a trick that Roderick does."

"We'd demonstrate," Allan broke in, "but taxidermy is a little disgusting and might spoil your audience's enjoyment of their cornflakes."

"Taxidermy?" the host asked, cautiously. He'd been warned that the Poes were not "ordinary" interviewees.

"And the second part of our two-pronged attack involved our much older friends, Clarence and Genevieve," Allan continued.

"Who?" the host asked, glancing across the studio to where Uncle Jack and Aunt Judith stood near the camera, watching.

"No, not them," Allan said.

"Clarence and Genevieve are dead," Edgar elaborated. "Whereas our aunt and uncle are very much alive, as you can see."

"Your helpers are dead?"

The twins nodded.

"They died helping you?"

"Oh, no," Edgar said. "They were dead all along."

Confused, the host sighed. It was no wonder the other two morning shows had turned down this interview.

But then the twins delivered a bombshell.

"We aren't actually here to talk about crime fighting," Allan said.

"No?" the host asked, cautiously.

"We're here to announce that, along with Em and Milly Dickinson—our costars in *A Tale of Poe* and the great-great-great-great grandnieces of Emily Dickinson—we have discovered the major portion of the lost treasure of the Lafitte brothers," Edgar announced. "Right here in New Orleans!"

"You're kidding!" the host cried.

The twins shook their heads. "Not just Pierre Lafitte's diary," Edgar said, revealing their role as museum vandals.

"But the gold, jewels . . . everything," Allan added.

"So it was you two who found Pierre Lafitte's diary and brought it to light?" the host asked, recalling the big news story of two days before.

"Along with the Dickinson twins," Allan reminded him.

"And where was the treasure hidden all these years?" the host asked.

"Tonight, at a special event at the New Orleans Pirate Museum, you'll find out all the details."

Before guiding Ms. Ellen Payne, curator of the New Orleans Pirate Museum, to the tomb of Lance de

Tremblement and the treasure hidden within, the Poe and Dickinson twins negotiated a good deal. They would donate to the museum 100 percent of their share of the treasure, provided the museum agreed to the following terms:

Two percent of the proceeds from the treasure would go to an organization that preserved original nineteenth-century poetry manuscripts (Em's idea).

Two percent would go to an organization that distributed computer technology and smartphones to underprivileged schools (Milly's idea).

Four percent would go to an organization that helped place orphaned children with good families (Edgar and Allan's idea).

Two percent would go to fight cruelty to animals (Roderick's idea).

And there had been other matters to work out. For example, there was the lock that the Poe and Dickinson twins had broken on the museum display case in which they'd placed Pierre Lafitte's incriminating diary. As a show of good faith, Ms. Payne agreed to overlook the minor offense.

"And the Pierre Lafitte wax figure is easily enough returned to its properly clothed state," she said.

But the boys were tough negotiators.

"We'll only take you to the treasure if you agree to leave him dressed as a convict forever," Edgar insisted.

"It's to serve as a reminder that Pierre was no swashbuckling hero but a scoundrel," Allan explained.

"We concur with Edgar and Allan," the Dickinson sisters chimed in.

Ms. Payne made a phone call to her board of directors, and, after a moment, agreed to all of the Poe and Dickinson demands.

She was not disappointed.

The treasure proved truly historic.

So that night at the New Orleans Pirate Museum's special event, the media, community, and pirate fans from all over the state gathered on the museum steps beneath a new banner:

When Ms. Payne announced from the podium, "Ladies and gentlemen, here they are, our treasure hunters: Em and Milly Dickinson, and Edgar and Allan Poe!" the crowd's cheers rose up like so many released spirits into the Louisiana night.

"And Roderick, too!" cried the boys.

And the cheers got even louder.

The next morning, the Poe family went downstairs to the lobby of the Pepper Tree Inn to say good-bye to the Dickinsons, who were going to the airport for a noon flight to the sunny beaches of Mexico. In contrast, the Poes planned to load up their Volvo wagon after lunch and start the long drive back to Baltimore. Edgar and Allan didn't mind. They looked forward to reuniting with their school friends. Well, they minded a little. . . .

They'd miss Em and Milly.

"Who'd have guessed that making a movie would be the *least* exciting part of this trip?" Em asked the boys as their respective parents and guardians checked out of the inn.

"Yeah," Edgar said lamely.

"True," Allan added uselessly.

Suddenly, the Poe twins couldn't think of a thing to say.

"You know what was the most exciting part of the trip for Em and me?" Milly asked.

"The ghosts?" Allan proposed.

"The treasure?" Edgar suggested.

"Meeting you two," Milly answered.

Em nodded in agreement.

Now Edgar and Allan couldn't get any words out at all—not even monosyllables.

The girls said nothing but just stood before them.

Are we supposed to hug good-bye? Edgar and Allan wondered.

But hugging girls wasn't all that simple for Edgar or Allan, even in the best of circumstances. They hadn't hugged many girls before (actually, discounting their mother and Aunt Judith, they'd hugged exactly zero). And now, in a lobby full of adults, this was far from the best of circumstances.

Was this an example of too much thinking about a simple thing?

That happens sometimes, even to smart boys (especially to smart boys).

The silence grew awkward.

The girls threw their arms around Edgar and Allan.

"Be safe," Milly whispered.

"We believe in you," Em whispered.

After a moment, the boys relaxed and allowed themselves to be hugged.

It was nice.

A little later, Edgar and Allan stood outside the Pepper Tree Inn watching the Dickinson family's cab pull away from the curb and into the slow-moving traffic. Uncle Jack came out of the lobby. He joined them, putting his arms around their shoulders.

"Last night, I did a little negotiating of my own with the museum, boys," he said.

Edgar and Allan looked up at him.

"What'd you get us, more beignets?" Allan teased him.

"Hey, that's a great idea," Uncle Jack said hungrily. "I wish I'd thought of it. Oh, well, I guess you two will have to settle for these."

He handed each boy a heavy gold doubloon. *Their own pirate treasure!*

"The museum people were happy for you kids to keep something," Uncle Jack explained.

"Em and Milly, too?"

Uncle Jack nodded.

The twins smiled and put the coins in their pockets. Their pirate-obsessed friend, David Litke, would love this.

Uncle Jack laughed. "Don't drop those in any vending machines. They're worth more than our house."

"Speaking of our house—" Edgar began.

"Let's go home, Uncle Jack," Allan continued.

"Baltimore it is, boys."

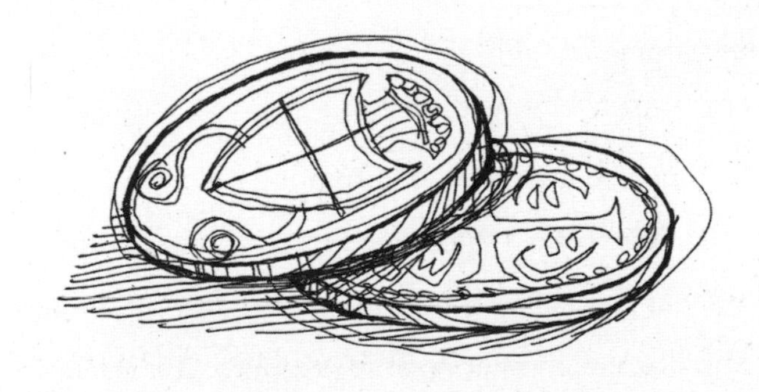

WHAT THE POE TWINS DID NOT KNOW . . .

A LETTER SENT THAT DAY:

IDENTITY SPECIALISTS, INC.

MOSCOW • SHANGHAI • ABU DHABI • BUENOS AIRES • CAPE TOWN • LAS VEGAS

Dear Professor Perry,

We hope you are pleased with our services so far.

Doctors report that your facial reconstruction surgery was a success and that you are on your way to a complete and unrecognizable recovery. Our document department is currently completing your new identity papers, including passport. All will be in order by the time you are ready to move on.

Here's to fresh starts!

Best Wishes,

Dr. Psufo

Founder and CEO

P.S. I hope you do not mind that I used your previous name in the salutation above. I take satisfaction in being the last to do so. I trust you will destroy this letter immediately after reading.

P.P.S. As requested, we have booked you an open airline ticket to Baltimore, Maryland, USA.

Mr. Poe in the Great Beyond

Mr. Poe didn't know what to expect of his first afternoon in the Animal Languages Division. Would it be as dull as watching alfalfa grow in a farmyard populated only by sleeping cows, dozing ducks, and sloppy pigs? Or would it be as stressful as being set to work with pen and paper on the sandy floor of the Roman Colosseum while roaring lions, growling bears, and maddened bulls circled maliciously? He didn't know which would be worse.

On the elevator ride down, he steeled himself for either.

When the elevator doors opened on the 121,347,935th floor, he was greeted by a surprise. The office looked almost indistinguishable from the working space he'd occupied for the past 180 or so years. There was the same foot-worn, institutional carpeting and fluorescent-lit cubicles. *Not so bad,* he thought. But as he started into the office, his box of desk supplies in his hands, he realized that seated in each cubicle was an animal murmuring to itself. Cows mooed, pigs oinked, and horses whinnied—all very quietly, thoughtfully.

"Most of them are suffering from writer's block," said someone behind him.

He turned.

It was Homer, the blind poet.

"But every once in a while, one of them will stumble across something quite worthwhile," he continued, motioning for Mr. Poe to draw nearer. "Did you know that one of the cows here named a famous lost continent?"

"No, I didn't know that."

"The continent was consumed in prehistory by the Atlantic Ocean."

"Moo?" Mr. Poe asked.

"Well, it's spelled 'M-u,' but this is where the name comes from," Homer answered.

"So what am *I* supposed to do here?"

Homer placed his hand on Mr. Poe's shoulder. "Just as these animals are exploring the possibilities of human language, admittedly with only rare success, you will explore the possibilities of animal language."

"Without *any* success . . ." Mr. Poe muttered.

"Now, let's be positive," Homer answered. He pointed in the general direction of an empty cubicle. "That's yours." He turned and walked away.

Discouraged, Mr. Poe set his box of supplies on the empty desk and took his seat. He expected the afternoon to consist of nothing but overheard lamb bleats, donkey brays, dog barks, and elephant trumpeting. But a mere five minutes after getting his desk set up to his liking, Mr. Poe was visited by, of all things, a pair of human beings.

Specifically, a gracious husband and wife.

Their apparel suggested they'd died in the first decades of Poe's own nineteenth century. Then he recognized them from his nephews' recent cemetery adventure.

"May we have a moment of your time?" the gentleman asked.

Mr. Poe stood and extended his hand. "Monsieur and Madame Du Valier, I presume?"

Clarence bowed; Genevieve curtseyed.

"We came to commend your excellent nephews, who represent your family so honorably down on earth," Genevieve said.

"We wouldn't be here without them," Clarence added.

"Here?" Mr. Poe asked, confused. "In the Animal Languages Division?"

"Oh, no," Clarence said, chuckling. "We're not writers . . . or, um, animals. No, we're going to be running the inn a million or so floors upstairs. Good food and spirits."

"And in honor of your family, we're going to rename our split pea soup," Genevieve said.

Mr. Poe narrowed his eyes questioningly.

"Split Poe." Clarence beamed.

"Isn't it remarkable how changing just one letter can make such a difference?" Genevieve observed.

"Yeah, great," Mr. Poe murmured, recalling the many times that one changed letter had scrambled the meaning of communiqués he'd smuggled down to his great-great-great-great grandnephews. "But thanks."

Twenty minutes later, Mr. Poe fell asleep with his head on his desk, having despaired of ever finding a way to communicate with his grandnephews using only the grunts of pigs or the clicking of dolphins.

In a dream, he found himself in a book-lined chamber, the setting of his most famous poem, "The Raven." He heard a tapping at the moonlit window. When he opened the shutters, a raven flew inside, perching on a sculpture of Athena, the Greek goddess of wisdom. Oddly, the dreaming Mr. Poe did not associate any of this with his poem but with real life. So when he asked the raven if he would ever find a way to help his grandnephews, and the raven replied, "Nevermore," it disturbed Mr. Poe so much that he woke up in a sweat.

Opening his eyes, he looked around his cubicle.

That's when he saw a real raven perched on the cubicle divider.

He couldn't stop himself from asking the same question that had tortured him in the dream. "Can I still be of help to my grandnephews?"

"Evermore!" the raven replied, before flying off to the other side of the Animal Languages Division.

Mr. Poe sighed in relief.

He had hope yet of warning Edgar and Allan that they were still not out of danger.

THE END

ACKNOWLEDGMENTS

Once again, my thanks to those who generously shared their talents with Edgar, Allan, and me. First, to my whip-smart editor, Sharyn November and my ever-insightful agent, Kelly Sonnack—you both went above and beyond the call of duty to help me find this story. To Sam Zuppardi and Eileen Savage, whose lively art and design infuse the book with delights. And much gratitude to Arte Johnson for literally giving voice to my words.

Also, thanks to my teachers, from elementary school through university, particularly Marie Dannenbring, Thomas Halleen, Anthony Corradino, Joseph Bell, Oakley Hall, Don Heiney, and Tom Massey—you are all in these pages (even if some of you have moved on to the celestial skyscraper to hang out with Mr. Poe).

Finally, thanks to my inspiring sons, Jonathan, Shane,

and Harlan. And to my wife, Julie, whose love makes fictional flights of fancy seem ordinary by comparison. —G.M.

Thanks firstly to Gordon, for writing all the words, and to my fantastic agent, Kelly, for having had the bright idea to match my pictures with them. To Sharyn, Nancy, Eileen, and the whole team at Viking, who brought everything together so brilliantly—and sent me transatlantic cookies!

To my parents, my grandparents, and Nic and Luisa, who offered so much support and encouragement. And finally to the lovely Jade, who has been there every step of the way, and who said "Yes!"—S.Z.

GORDON McALPINE is the author of the first Poe Boys misadventure, *The Tell-Tale Start*. He is also the author of adult novels ranging from magical realism to hard-boiled literary mysteries. He lives with his wife in Southern California.

Visit the Poe twins (and the Dickinson sisters) at www.The-poes.net.

Visit Gordon at www.gordonmcalpine.com.

SAM ZUPPARDI spent much of his childhood drawing complicated treasure maps, although he never actually owned any proper pirate treasure.

He now lives in York, England—a particularly good city for ghost walks. He illustrated *The Tell-Tale Start*, and his first picture book, *The Nowhere Box*, is available now. Visit www.samzuppardi.com for more.

WITHDRAWN

For Every Individual...

Renew by Phone
269-5222

Renew on the Web
www.indypl.org

For General Library Information
please call 275-4100